THE BROKEN NIGHT

NEW SCIONS: BOOK ONE

C.L. STEGALL

STUDIO VALENSI

Table of Contents

COPYRIGHT

DEDICATION

FOR MONA

CHAPTER 1: NORMAL FALTERS

The vinyl mat beneath Alexis Rain's bare feet absorbed the impact as she pivoted, her blonde ponytail whipping through the air like a weapon of its own. Across from her, Jamie Keats shifted his weight, brown curls falling into those green eyes that seemed to catch everything, including the series of strikes she was about to unleash.

"Think. Visualize your moves, Alexis-kun," Sensei's voice cut through the humid air of the Eastern Light Dojo. Even after eight years of training, the old man still used that familiar tone with her, the one that suggested she was capable of more than she was showing.

Alexis feinted left, then drove forward with a combination that should have caught Keats off-guard. Should have. Instead, he flowed backward like water, blocking each strike with an ease that made her teeth clench. The bastard was grinning again, that lopsided smirk that said he knew exactly what she was thinking before she thought it.

"Keats-san," Sensei continued, his attention shifting to her sparring partner, "Focus. Kumite is not meant to be amusing. It is meant to test your abilities and awareness."

"Sorry, Sensei," Keats replied, but the grin never left his face as he ducked under Alexis's roundhouse kick and swept her supporting leg.

She hit the mat with a grunt that echoed through the dojo, her eidetic memory instantly cataloging the move—the angle of his approach, the timing of the sweep, the way he'd shifted his weight to compensate for her counterattack that hadn't come. She'd file it away with the thousands of other details her mind collected without her permission, another piece of data in the vast library that had made her feel like a freak since she was nine years old.

"Not really fair using that perfect memory of yours, Al," Keats said, offering her a hand up. "You know me too well."

Alexis ignored the hand and rolled to her feet in one fluid motion. She dropped into a defensive stance, noting how the other students—ranging from thirteen to thirty-two—watched them with wide eyes. They always did. She and Keats moved faster than the others, hit harder, recovered quicker. It should have bothered her more than it did. "So? Surprise me."

The words had barely left her mouth when something crawled up her spine like ice water. The sensation hit her with such force that her concentration shattered, and in that split second of distraction, Keats's fist connected with her solar plexus.

Air exploded from her lungs as she staggered backward, but it wasn't the pain that made her heart race. It was the feeling of being watched. Studied. Evaluated by eyes that didn't belong in this place, at this time, with these people who thought karate class was the most dangerous thing in their lives.

"Yame!" Sensei called, stopping the match. He moved between them; his weathered face creased with concern. "Alexis-kun, your focus was elsewhere. In a real confrontation, such distraction could be fatal."

She nodded, still searching the room for whatever had triggered that primal alert system in her brain. The plate glass window that faced the street showed nothing but afternoon pedestrians and parked cars. No one lurking. No one watching. But the feeling persisted, like an itch between her shoulder blades.

"Sorry," she managed, bowing to Keats and then to Sensei. "I thought I saw—"

Her phone rang on the bench behind her, the specific ringtone she'd set for emergencies only cutting through her explanation. She was just close enough to see the photo of her dad, Charles, fill the screen. She loved that picture of her father in his hard hat at one of his construction sites, smiling at something beyond the camera's range. if she remembered correctly, and of course she did, that had been her mom, Elizabeth, making some off-color remark to get him to smile.

"I need to take this," she said, bowing to the both of them and stepping off the mat.

"Alexis?" Her father's voice carried an urgency that made her stomach clench. Charles Rain didn't do urgent. He did methodical, careful, planned. He was the kind of man who scheduled his spontaneity.

"Dad? What's wrong?"

"I need you to come home. Now."

"But class isn't—"

"Now, pumpkin. Please."

The line went dead.

Alexis stared at the phone for a moment, that crawling sensation between her shoulder blades intensifying. Around her, the dojo continued its normal rhythm— students practicing kata, the sharp crack of boards breaking, Sensei's voice guiding a newer student through basic blocks. Normal sounds. Normal sights. So why did everything feel like it was tilting sideways?

"Al?" Keats appeared beside her, sweat still beading on his forehead. "Everything okay?"

"I have to go." She was already moving toward the changing room, muscle memory taking over while her mind tried to process the wrongness in her father's voice. "Dad wants me home."

"Want me to drive you?"

"I've got Betsy." She grabbed her gear bag from the bench, not bothering to change out of her gi. Whatever had spooked her father badly enough to interrupt karate class, something he'd never done in eight years, wasn't going to wait for her to shower and change.

"Alexis." Sensei's voice stopped her at the door. "Remember what we discussed about awareness. Trust your instincts. They are often more reliable than your conscious mind."

She nodded, though his words only added to the unease crawling through her chest. Outside, the late afternoon sun hit her like a physical blow, and she squinted against the glare as she jogged toward her BMW.

The key fob beeped, and she slid behind the wheel, her hands shaking slightly as she started the engine. Betsy purred to life, all German engineering and leather seats that still held that new car smell Keats loved to tease her about. The normalcy of it should have been comforting. Instead, it felt like putting on a costume that no longer fit.

As she pulled out of the parking lot, Alexis caught a glimpse of movement in her rear-view mirror. A figure in dark clothing, standing motionless on the sidewalk while everyone else flowed around him like water around a stone. She craned her neck to get a better look, but a delivery truck blocked her view and, when it passed, the figure was gone.

Her hands tightened on the steering wheel as she navigated the familiar streets toward home. Mount Pleasant had always felt like a way station to her, a temporary stop between wherever she'd been and wherever she was going. The tree-lined streets and modest houses represented safety, predictability, the kind of life where the biggest crisis was whether to take AP Chemistry or AP Physics senior year. For both of which she had already finished finals.

But as Betsy's engine hummed beneath her, carrying her toward whatever had put that tone in her father's voice, Alexis couldn't shake the feeling that her safe, predictable life was about to become something else entirely.

The Rain house sat at the end of College Street like a postcard from suburban America—two stories of cream-colored siding, black shutters, and a wraparound porch that her mother had spent countless weekends perfecting. Elizabeth's flower beds blazed with late spring color; each bloom precisely placed according to some master plan that existed only in her event planner's mind.

Alexis pulled into the driveway and sat for a moment, studying the house that had been her anchor for eighteen years. Nothing looked different. The porch swing still hung at the exact angle her mother preferred. The morning paper still sat folded beside the front door because her father refused to bring it in until evening, claiming it was bad luck to read the news before sunset. Even her perch on the roof was empty and still as it always was without her.

Normal. Everything looked perfectly, impossibly normal.

So why did it feel like she was looking at a movie set?

The front door opened before she reached the porch steps, and Charles Rain emerged like a man walking underwater. His normally crisp button-down shirt was wrinkled, his graying hair mussed as if he'd been running his hands through it. But it was his eyes that stopped her cold—red-rimmed and hollow, like someone had scooped out everything that made him her father and left behind an empty shell.

"Dad?" The word came out smaller than she intended.

He opened his arms, and she fell into them the way she had when she was six and afraid of thunderstorms. His embrace felt different somehow—tighter, more desperate, as if he was trying to hold onto something that was already slipping away.

"I'm sorry, pumpkin," he whispered into her hair. "I'm so sorry."

And at that moment, before he said the words that would shatter her world into before and after, Alexis Rain understood that normal was a luxury she would never have again.

The words hit Alexis like physical blows, each syllable driving deeper into her chest until she couldn't breathe. Car accident. Elizabeth. Didn't make it. The phrases bounced around her skull, refusing to arrange themselves into anything that made sense.

Her mother was supposed to be in Charlotte tonight, staying at the Marriott downtown after her late meeting with the Japanese investors. She was supposed to call at eight-thirty to say goodnight, the way she always did when business kept her away. She was supposed to come home tomorrow morning with coffee from that little place on Trade Street and stories about difficult clients who didn't understand the difference between elegant and gaudy.

She was not supposed to be dead.

"The police said it happened around dawn," Charles continued, his voice mechanical, like he was reading from a script. "On that stretch of road just before the event center. They think she swerved to avoid something, maybe a deer."

Alexis pulled back to study her father's face, searching for some sign that this was an elaborate, cruel joke. But Charles didn't joke about serious things. He barely joked about anything. And the devastation carved into his features was too raw, too complete to be anything but genuine.

"Where is she?" The question came out flat, emotionless. She should be crying. She should be screaming. She should be doing something other than standing here like a statue while her father fell apart in front of her.

"Hospital. For now." He scrubbed his hands over his face. "There'll be... arrangements to make. Viewing. Funeral. Your mother had opinions about these things."

Elizabeth Rain had opinions about everything. Which flowers for which season, which fork to use for salad, which colleges would best suit a daughter with a photographic memory and no clear direction in life. The thought of making decisions about Elizabeth's funeral without Elizabeth's input seemed impossible, like trying to paint a portrait with half the colors missing.

"I should call Keats," Alexis said, because the silence between them was becoming unbearable. "And Katy."

"Already done. They're on their way."

Of course they were. Jamie Keats and his mother had been fixtures in the Rain household since Alexis was six years old. Katy worked nights at the hospital, single-handedly raising a son who was too smart for his own good, while Elizabeth had become a guiding figure for them both. The two women had formed a bond that transcended friendship, becoming something closer to sisters.

Katy would be devastated.

The sound of tires on gravel announced their arrival. Through the front window, Alexis watched Keats unfold himself from the passenger seat of his mother's Honda Civic, his face grim in a way that didn't belong on someone who still had twenty-three freckles across his nose. Katy emerged from the driver's side, her nurse's scrubs wrinkled from a double shift, her dark hair escaping from its ponytail.

They moved toward the house like mourners approaching a grave.

"Hey," Keats said when Charles opened the door. It was such an inadequate word for the situation, but what else was there? Alexis appreciated that he didn't try to fill the silence with empty condolences or meaningless reassurances that everything would be okay.

Katy wrapped Alexis in a hug that smelled of hospital antiseptic and lavender shampoo. "I'm so sorry, sweetheart."

The tears should have come then. Should have exploded out of her in great, wrenching sobs that purged the grief and shock from her system. Instead, Alexis felt nothing but a vast, echoing emptiness where her emotions should have been. She hugged Katy back because it was expected, made the right noises because it was polite, but inside she remained frozen.

"Sit," Katy ordered, guiding both Alexis and Charles to the living room couch. "I'll make coffee."

She disappeared toward the kitchen with the efficiency of someone who had dealt with crises before, leaving the three of them arranged in a tableau of grief. Charles stared at his hands. Keats perched on the edge of the coffee table, close enough to reach out if needed but far enough away not to crowd. Alexis catalogued every detail of the room—the way the afternoon light slanted through the blinds, creating prison bar shadows on the hardwood floor; the faint scent of Elizabeth's vanilla candles; the stack of event planning magazines on the side table that would never be read.

Her perfect memory preserved it all with ruthless efficiency, storing away this moment when her life split cleanly into before and after.

"We'll set up the viewing later this week," Charles said eventually. "I think the funeral will likely be Thursday or Friday morning at the Methodist church. Your mother... she had everything planned out. Filed away in her desk with all the other important papers."

Of course she did. Elizabeth Rain planned everything, from dinner parties to grocery lists to, apparently, her own death. The woman who color-coded her calendar and kept backup plans for her backup plans had naturally considered her own mortality with the same systematic thoroughness she applied to everything else.

"What do you need us to do?" Keats asked.

"Nothing. Just... Take care of each other." Charles's voice cracked on the last word. "Liz thought of everything. We've gone over a dozen times in the past few years. Casket, flowers, music, what she wanted me to say. It's all there in black and white, organized by priority." With that, a tiny smile crept over his face, so many memories of his wife and her tell-tell ways. Just as quickly, the smile faded into the blank stare of a broken man lost in thoughts he truly did not want to think.

The sound of the coffee maker gurgling to life drifted in from the kitchen, normal and domestic and completely at odds with the conversation happening in the living room. Alexis found herself focusing on that sound, using it as an anchor while everything else threatened to drift away.

"The police give you anything other than the swerving?" Katy said, returning with a tray of steaming mugs. Charles only shook his head. None of that really mattered anymore, anyway.

Alexis accepted the coffee without really seeing it, the ceramic warm against her palms. "She was fine yesterday. Normal. Excited about the presentation."

But even as she said it, she wasn't sure. When was the last time she'd really looked at her mother? Really listened to what she was saying instead of just cataloguing the words for later reference? Elizabeth moved through their house like a force of nature, organizing and planning and managing, but when had Alexis last seen her as a person instead of just... background?

The guilt hit her like a physical blow, doubling her over with its intensity. While she'd been worried about college applications and karate tests and whether Keats liked her as more than a friend, her mother had been driving through the pre-dawn darkness toward whatever had made her swerve off that road.

"Don't," Keats said quietly, and she realized he was reading her face with the uncanny accuracy that had defined their friendship. "Don't blame yourself for not seeing something that probably wasn't there to see."

But that was the problem. With her memory, there was always something there to see. Every conversation, every expression, every tiny detail was preserved with photographic clarity. If she'd bothered to pay attention, if she'd cared about something other than her own problems, maybe she would have noticed if anything had been bothering Elizabeth. Maybe she could have said something, done something, changed the trajectory of events that led to a dawn collision on an empty road.

"The services will be later this week," Charles repeated to Katy, as if saying it often enough would make it real. "After... Folks can come back here for..." He gestured vaguely at the house. "Whatever people do."

Elizabeth would have known what people did. She would have had caterers lined up, flowers arranged, a timeline coordinating every detail from the opening prayer to the final goodbye. Without her, they were all just stumbling around in the dark, making it up as they went along.

Alexis set down her untouched coffee and stood abruptly. "I need some air."

She walked out before anyone could object, letting the screen door slam behind her. The front porch offered no relief from the weight pressing down on her chest, so she kept walking, down the steps and across the yard to the old oak tree where she and Keats had built a fort when they were eight.

The rope swing still hung from the lowest branch, weathered now but functional. Elizabeth had insisted Charles test it every spring to make sure it would hold their weight, even though they'd both outgrown the need for backyard entertainment years ago.

Just one more thing her mother had thought to plan for.

Alexis sank onto the swing, letting it sway gently under her weight. From there, she could see into the kitchen window where Katy was washing the coffee mugs with the kind of mechanical precision that kept grief at bay. Charles sat at the kitchen table; shoulders bowed under an invisible weight. Keats stood in the doorway between kitchen and living room, clearly torn between staying with her father and following her outside.

They all looked like actors playing parts in a play none of them had auditioned for.

A movement at the edge of her vision made her turn toward the street. A figure stood beneath the streetlamp that had just flickered on in the gathering dusk—medium height, wearing what looked like a long trench coat despite the late spring warmth. Too far away to make out details, but close enough to trigger that same crawling sensation she'd felt at the dojo.

Alexis blinked, and the figure was gone.

CHAPTER 2: FIRST CONTACT

The funeral home's parking lot stretched like a black sea under the fluorescent lights, filled with cars that belonged to people who had known Elizabeth Rain as more than just a name in an obituary. Alexis sat in the passenger seat of her father's Escalade, watching mourners stream toward the entrance in their respectful dark clothing, and felt like she was observing the proceedings through bulletproof glass.

Two days had passed since Charles had delivered the news that split her world in half. Two days of phone calls and casseroles and well-meaning neighbors who spoke in hushed tones about God's plan and being in a better place. Two days of feeling like she was drowning in other people's grief while her own remained locked away somewhere she couldn't reach.

"Ready?" Charles asked, though the question was pointless. Ready implied choice, and choice implied the luxury of walking away. None of them had that option.

The funeral director had done his job well. Elizabeth looked peaceful in the mahogany casket, her blonde hair arranged perfectly, her hands folded over the navy dress she'd worn to Alexis's high school awards ceremony. Someone had applied makeup with a heavier hand than Elizabeth ever would have used in life, but the overall effect was serene. Restful. All the euphemisms people used when they couldn't bring themselves to say dead.

Alexis stood beside the casket and waited for tears that refused to come. Around her, friends and family members wept openly, sharing memories and offering comfort to each other. She catalogued their words, their expressions, their gestures, filing everything away in the vast storage facility of her mind while feeling nothing but that same hollow emptiness.

"She was so proud of you," Mrs. Henderson from next door said, squeezing Alexis's hand with fingers that smelled of arthritis cream and rose perfume. "Always talking about how smart you were, how you were going to do great things."

Alexis nodded and made the appropriate noises, but the words bounced off her like arrows off armor. Elizabeth had been proud. Elizabeth had talked about her future. Elizabeth had done a thousand things that were now frozen in past tense, preserved only in the memories of people who had bothered to pay attention.

Keats appeared at her elbow, solid and reassuring in his black suit that made him look older than eighteen. "You okay?"

"Fine." The lie came easily, practiced over the past two days until it felt almost true.

"Liar." But he said it gently, without judgment. "You haven't cried yet."

"So?"

"So, you loved her. And people who love their mothers usually cry when they die."

The accusation in his voice was mild, but it hit her like a slap. "Maybe I'm not most people."

"Maybe." He studied her face with those too-perceptive green eyes. "Or maybe you're scared that if you start, you won't be able to stop."

Before she could answer, a ripple of awareness swept through the room like a cold wind. Her head turned toward the entrance as conversations faltered without reason then started up again in the same manner. Alexis felt that familiar crawling sensation between her shoulder blades that had become as persistent as her own heartbeat.

He stood just inside the doorway, perfectly still while the crowd moved around him as if he was completely unnoticed. The same figure she'd glimpsed outside the dojo, outside her house, hovering at the edges of her vision for the past two days. Up close, he was younger than she'd expected—maybe thirty, with sharp cheekbones and dark hair slicked back from a face that belonged in a Renaissance painting. His expensive charcoal suit and black fedora would have looked ridiculous on anyone else, but on him they seemed natural, as if he'd stepped out of another era entirely.

"Friend of your mother's?" Keats asked, following her gaze.

"I don't think so." Alexis watched the stranger navigate the crowd with fluid grace, accepting condolences from people who seemed to know him, though she was certain she'd never seen him before in her life. "But he's been watching me."

"Watching you how?"

"Everywhere I go. Like he's waiting for something."

Keats's expression shifted from concern to something harder, more protective. "Want me to—"

"No." She caught his arm before he could move. "I'll handle it."

The stranger had reached the casket now, standing with his head bowed as if paying his respects. But his eyes weren't on Elizabeth. They were on Alexis, studying her with an intensity that made her skin crawl. When their gazes met, he smiled—a small, knowing expression that suggested they shared a secret she wasn't aware of yet.

He approached with the confident stride of someone who had never been told no, never been denied access to anything he wanted. People stepped aside to let him pass, though Alexis noticed they seemed unconscious of the movement, as if they were responding to some subliminal command.

"Alexis." His voice was soft and melodious, with an accent she couldn't place. British, maybe, or something older. "I've been looking forward to meeting you."

"Have we met?" She kept her tone neutral, though every instinct screamed at her to run.

"Not formally. But I feel as though I know you quite well. You may call me Pitts." He glanced toward the casket, and something flickered across his features—distaste, perhaps, or impatience. "A tragic loss. Though perhaps not unexpected."

The words hit her like a physical blow. "Excuse me?"

"Car accidents are so common, aren't they? Especially on those winding roads where a moment's distraction can prove... fatal." His smile widened, revealing teeth that were too white, too perfect. "One might almost call it convenient."

Heat flooded Alexis's chest, burning away the numbness that had protected her for the past two days. "Who the hell are you?"

"Careful." His voice dropped to a whisper that somehow carried more menace than a shout. "We wouldn't want to cause a scene at your dear mother's viewing."

She glanced around and realized he was right. Despite the intensity of their conversation, no one else seemed to be paying attention. Keats stood less than ten feet away, but his gaze had gone distant, unfocused, as if he were looking through her rather than at her.

"What did you do to them?"

"Nothing permanent. I simply prefer privacy for important conversations." He stepped closer, invading her personal space with the casual arrogance of a predator who had never encountered effective resistance. "And this conversation is very important indeed."

"I don't know what you want—"

"I want you to stop pretending." The pleasantness dropped from his voice like a discarded mask. "Stop playing the grieving daughter to these sheep who wouldn't recognize real power if it bit them. You're special, Alexis. More special than you can possibly imagine. And it's time you started acting like it."

"You're insane."

"Am I?" He tilted his head, studying her like a particularly interesting specimen. "Tell me, have you noticed anything... unusual about yourself lately? Moments where reality seems to bend around you? Dreams that feel more real than waking life? A growing sense that you don't quite belong in this little suburban paradise?"

Each question hit its mark with surgical precision. The dreams of obsidian doors and starlit chambers. The way shadows seemed to welcome her, wrapping around her like old friends. The constant feeling that she was sleepwalking through a life that belonged to someone else.

"How do you—"

"Know?" He smiled again, and this time there was something almost paternal in the expression. "Because I've been watching you for a very long time. Waiting for the right moment to make contact. Waiting for you to be ready to hear the truth about what you really are."

"Which is?"

"The daughter of something far greater than these mortals could comprehend. The inheritor of power that makes their petty concerns irrelevant." He gestured toward the mourners around them, and his lip curled with barely concealed disgust. "You weren't meant to waste away in this suffocating normalcy, pretending to grieve for a woman who was never really your mother."

The words exploded in her chest like shrapnel. "Don't you dare—"

"Elizabeth Rain was a placeholder. A convenient vessel to carry you until you were old enough to claim your birthright." His voice grew softer, more persuasive. "Deep down, you've always known you were different. Special. Destined for something more than this mundane existence."

He was right, and that terrified her more than anything else he could have said. She had always felt displaced, like an actor reading lines from a script she'd never seen. But Elizabeth had been real. Elizabeth's love had been real. Even if the biology was complicated, the bond they'd shared—

"She loved me," Alexis said, hating how small her voice sounded.

"Perhaps. In her limited way." He shrugged, dismissing eighteen years of memories with casual indifference. "But love isn't enough to change what you are. What you're becoming. The power growing inside you won't be contained much longer, and when it breaks free..." He leaned closer, his breath warm against her ear. "Well. Let's just say your little suburban paradise won't survive the revelation."

Images flashed through her mind—the weirdness of her perfect memory, the way shadows seemed to bend toward her in the darkness, the growing sense that the world was made of paper and she was made of fire.

"What do you want from me?"

"Nothing you won't eventually give willingly." He straightened, adjusting his fedora with practiced elegance. "I want you to embrace your nature instead of fighting it. I want you to stop wasting your potential on these insects who will never understand what you're capable of. And I want you to remember that when the time comes to choose sides, there are consequences for choosing poorly."

"Choose sides in what?"

"You'll know soon enough." He glanced toward the casket again, and this time she caught the full force of his contempt. "Your dear departed Elizabeth couldn't protect you forever. She knew this day would come—they all did. The signs were becoming too obvious to ignore. A few more months and even these blind fools would have started asking uncomfortable questions."

The implication hit her like ice water. "Are you saying she didn't die in an accident?"

"I'm saying that accidents have a way of happening to people who stand between extraordinary children and their destinies." His smile returned, cold and sharp as winter starlight. "Elizabeth Rain served her purpose. She kept you safe and hidden until you were old enough to survive the revelation. But that phase of your life is over now, whether you accept it or not."

Rage built in her chest, hot and bright and completely foreign. She'd never felt anger like this before—clean and pure and powerful enough to remake the world. The air around her began to shimmer, and she felt something vast and terrible stirring in the depths of her soul.

"I wouldn't, if I were you," the stranger said mildly. "Not here. Not surrounded by so many fragile lives that could be snuffed out by a moment's loss of control."

The threat was clear, and it doused her anger like cold water on flame. She looked around at the mourners—Keats still frozen in place, her father accepting condolences near the guest book, Katy arranging flowers with mechanical precision. All of them trapped in whatever spell this creature had woven, all of them vulnerable to whatever power was trying to claw its way out of her chest.

"Who are you?" she whispered.

"Like I said, you can call me Pitts." He tipped his hat with mock courtesy. "And I'll be seeing you again very soon. When you're ready to stop playing house with these mortals and start living up to your potential."

He turned to leave, then paused at the door. "Oh, and Alexis? I'd be very careful about who you trust in the days to come. Your father kept secrets from you for eighteen years. What makes you think he's told you everything you should know?"

The words hung in the air like poison gas as he walked away. Around her, the mourners began to stir as if waking from a collective dream. Keats blinked and shook his head, his gaze focusing on her face with laser intensity.

"Al? What's wrong? You look like you've seen a ghost."

She opened her mouth to tell him about Pitts, about the impossible conversation and the terrible implications, but the words died in her throat. How could she explain that her mother's death might not have been an accident? That she was apparently something other than human? That a stranger in an expensive suit had just threatened everyone she cared about?

"Nothing," she said instead, the lie bitter on her tongue. "Just tired."

But as she looked toward the entrance where Pitts had disappeared, she knew that nothing would ever be simple again. Whatever had been growing inside her for the past eighteen years was about to break free, and when it did, the normal world she'd always felt displaced from would shatter completely.

The only question was whether she'd be able to protect the people she loved when it happened.

Or whether they'd become acceptable casualties in whatever apparent war it seemed Pitts was trying to recruit her for.

The reception at the Rain house felt like a wake for normalcy itself. Neighbors clustered in the living room, their voices hushed as they shared memories of Elizabeth's tireless volunteer work and legendary dinner parties. The kitchen overflowed with casseroles and condolence cards, testaments to a life well-lived and deeply mourned. But beneath the surface civility, Alexis felt the electric tension that preceded a thunderstorm.

She moved through the crowd like a sleepwalker, accepting hugs and murmured sympathies while her mind replayed every word of her conversation with Pitts. The implications twisted through her thoughts like poison, contaminating every interaction with the possibility that nothing was what it seemed.

Charles stood near the fireplace, fielding questions about the service with mechanical politeness. But Alexis noticed how his eyes never quite met anyone's gaze, how his hands trembled slightly when he thought no one was looking. The man who had raised her for eighteen years suddenly felt like a stranger wearing her father's face.

Your father kept secrets from you for eighteen years. What makes you think he's told you everything you should know?

"More coffee?" Katy appeared at her elbow, holding a steaming pot with the efficiency of someone who had learned to stay busy during grief. Her nurse's training showed in the way she monitored the room, checking on Charles, making sure elderly Mrs. Patterson had a place to sit, orchestrating comfort with subtle precision.

"Thanks." Alexis accepted a fresh cup she didn't want, using it as a prop to avoid conversation. The bitter liquid tasted like ashes, but it gave her hands something to do.

"Your mother would be proud," Katy continued, her voice carefully neutral. "The way you're holding up. Supporting your father. It can't be easy."

The words were meant as comfort, but they scraped against Alexis's raw nerves like sandpaper. *Holding up.* As if her inability to cry, to properly grieve, was somehow admirable instead of deeply wrong. As if the numbness that had settled over her like armor was strength rather than dysfunction.

"She wasn't really my mother, was she?" The question escaped before Alexis could stop it, quiet enough that only Katy could hear.

Katy's carefully composed expression cracked, revealing something that might have been fear. "Sweetheart, what a thing to say. Of course she was your mother. Why on earth would you say something like that?"

"Something. Some secrets untold. Something dangerous." Alexis set down her coffee cup with enough force to rattle the saucer. "And, apparently, I need to have a serious conversation with my father."

"Alexis—"

"Did you know?" The words came out sharper than intended, drawing glances from nearby mourners. Alexis lowered her voice but didn't back down. "When I was growing up, did you know I wasn't really Elizabeth's daughter?"

Katy's silence was answer enough. Her expression said everything she did not.

The betrayal hit Alexis like a physical blow, stealing her breath and making her vision blur around the edges. Not just Charles, then. Not just Elizabeth. This woman who had been like a second mother to her, who had bandaged scraped knees and listened to teenage complaints and taught her to drive when Charles was too nervous to do it himself—she had been part of the conspiracy too.

"Who else knows?" Alexis whispered.

"It wasn't—" Katy started, then stopped, her nurse's training warring with maternal instinct. "It's complicated."

"Everything's complicated now." Alexis turned away before the conversation could continue, pushing through the crowd toward the relative sanctuary of the kitchen.

Keats was there, leaning against the counter with a plate of untouched food in his hands. He looked up as she entered, and something in his expression told her he'd been waiting for her to crack.

"Want to get out of here?" he asked without preamble.

"Yes." The word came out with more desperation than she'd intended. "Please."

They slipped out the back door without saying goodbye, escaping into the twilight that had settled over the neighborhood like a familiar blanket. The air still held the warmth of late spring, but underneath it lurked the promise of summer storms and change.

"So," Keats said as they walked toward the old playground at the end of the street. "Want to tell me what really happened at the viewing?"

Alexis kicked a loose stone, watching it skitter across the asphalt. How could she explain an encounter that defied rational explanation? How could she describe a conversation that had turned her entire world upside down?

"Someone was there. Someone who shouldn't have been."

"The guy in the suit?"

She stopped walking. "You saw him?"

"Hard to miss. He stuck out like a sore thumb." Keats's expression grew troubled. "But here's the weird thing—for about ten minutes there, I couldn't focus on anything else. Like I was watching a movie with the sound turned down. And then suddenly he was gone and everything snapped back to normal."

The confirmation that she hadn't imagined the encounter brought no relief. If anything, it made everything worse. Whatever Pitts was, whatever he could do, he was real enough to affect other people. Real enough to make threats that carried actual weight.

"He knew things," she said finally. "About me. About my family. Things he shouldn't have been able to know."

"What kind of things?"

They had reached the playground, a collection of swings and slides that had entertained countless neighborhood children over the years. Alexis settled onto one of the swings, the chains creaking under her weight as she tried to organize her thoughts into something coherent.

"He said Elizabeth wasn't really my mother. That she was just... keeping me safe until I was old enough to handle the truth about what I really am." The words tasted strange in her mouth, like speaking a foreign language she barely understood.

Keats lowered himself onto the swing beside her, his expression serious. "And what are you? According to this guy?"

"I don't know. Something not entirely human." She laughed, but there was no sense of humor in the sound. "God, listen to me. I sound insane."

"You sound scared." His voice was gentle, without judgment. "And considering the week you've had, that seems pretty reasonable." He hesitated for but a second. "Then, again, I don't think I've ever actually seen you scared."

"He implied that my mother's death wasn't an accident."

The words hung between them like a live wire, dangerous and crackling with potential. Keats went very still, his hands tightening on the swing's chains.

"Implied how?"

"He said accidents have a way of happening to people who stand between extraordinary children and their destinies. That Elizabeth served her purpose, but that phase of my life was over." Her voice cracked on the last words. "Jesus, Keats. What if he killed her?"

"Hey." Keats's swing moved closer, close enough that he could reach out and take her hand. "Don't go down that road. Not without proof."

"But what if—"

"*What if* doesn't help anyone. *What if* drives you crazy." His grip tightened, anchoring her to the present moment. "Besides, you're forgetting something important."

"Which is?"

"You said he seemed like he was trying to recruit you for something. People don't generally recruit by murdering the target's family. That's more of a 'create an enemy' strategy than a 'make an ally' one."

The logic was sound, but it did nothing to ease the cold dread settling in her stomach. "Then why is she dead?"

"I don't know. Maybe it really was an accident. Maybe whoever this guy represents decided the time was right and engineered something that looked accidental. Or maybe—" He paused, clearly reluctant to voice the thought.

"Maybe what?"

"Maybe she found out about their plans and tried to stop them."

The possibility hit her like a sledgehammer. Elizabeth, discovering some threat to her daughter and attempting to intervene. Elizabeth, dying not because she was an obstacle to Alexis's destiny but because she was trying to protect her from it.

"I have to know the truth," Alexis said. "About all of it. What I am, what this guy wants from me, what really happened to my mom."

"We," Keats corrected. "We have to know the truth. You're not doing this alone."

"It's dangerous. You heard what I said about the guy making people freeze up. What if next time—"

"Next time I'll be ready for it." His jaw set with stubborn determination. "Al, we've been best friends for twelve years. You think I'm going to bail on you now just because things got weird?"

"This isn't weird, Keats. This is… supernatural. Impossible. The kind of thing that gets people killed."

"Then we'd better be smart about it." He stood up, pulling her with him. "Starting with getting answers from someone who actually knows what's going on."

"Like who?"

"Like your father."

The suggestion made her stomach clench. Charles, who had apparently lied to her for eighteen years. Charles, who might know exactly what kind of danger she was in and had chosen to keep her in the dark. Charles, who was currently hosting Elizabeth's wake while harboring secrets that could explain everything.

"What if he won't tell us?"

Keats's smile was sharp and humorless. "Then we'll make him."

They walked back toward the house in silence, but it was a different kind of quiet than before. Purposeful. Determined. The numbness that had protected Alexis for the past two days was burning away, replaced by something harder and more dangerous.

She was done being a victim of other people's secrets. Done accepting half-truths and careful omissions as protection. Whatever was happening to her, whatever power was growing inside her, she was going to face it with open eyes.

Even if the truth destroyed everything she thought she knew about herself and the people she loved.

The house came into view, its windows glowing warmly against the darkening sky. From the outside, it looked peaceful, normal, safe. But Alexis knew now that safety was an illusion, and normal was a luxury she could no longer afford.

Inside those walls waited answers she wasn't sure she was ready to hear.

But ready or not, it was time to stop hiding from her destiny.

CHAPTER 3: AWAKENING

The last mourner's car pulled away from the curb just after ten o'clock, leaving the Rain house feeling hollow and too large, like a theater after the final curtain call. Alexis watched from the living room window as the taillights disappeared around the corner, carrying with them the last pretense of normalcy.

Charles moved through the aftermath with mechanical efficiency, collecting coffee cups and folding chairs with the same methodical precision he brought to his construction projects. But his movements were sluggish, weighed down by grief and something else—something that might have been guilt.

"Dad." Alexis's voice cut through the silence like a blade. "We need to talk."

He froze in the middle of stacking dessert plates, his shoulders tensing as if bracing for impact. "It's been a long day, pumpkin. Maybe we should—"

"Now."

The word carried more authority than she'd intended, and Charles turned to face her with something that looked suspiciously like fear in his eyes. Jamie flanked her left side, his presence solid and reassuring, while Katy hovered near the kitchen doorway like she was calculating escape routes.

"About what?" Charles asked, though his careful tone suggested he already knew.

"About the stranger at the viewing. About the things he said. About the lies you've been telling me for eighteen years." Each accusation hit its mark, and she watched her father flinch as if she were throwing stones.

"Alexis, I don't know what you think you heard—"

"He knew, Dad. He knew about my real mother, about the circumstances of my birth, about secrets you've been keeping. So, either you told him, or someone else did, or—" She paused, letting the implication hang in the air. "Or he was there when it happened."

The color drained from Charles's face, leaving him looking every one of his fifty-three years. He sank into his recliner like a man who had been carrying a heavy load for too long and finally found permission to set it down.

"What did he tell you?" His voice came out barely above a whisper.

"That Elizabeth wasn't my real mother. That I'm something more than human. That her death might not have been an accident." Alexis perched on the edge of the couch, every muscle coiled for action. "Now it's your turn. Tell me what really happened eighteen years ago."

Charles closed his eyes, and for a moment she thought he might refuse to answer. Then he drew a shaky breath and began to speak, his words measured and careful as if he were defusing a bomb.

"I never learned her name. She said names had power, and she couldn't risk giving me hers." He opened his eyes, staring at some point beyond the far wall. "I was in Chicago for a week, overseeing the concrete pour for a high-rise project. Big job, lots of pressure, and I was working sixteen-hour days trying to keep everything on schedule."

"And?" Jamie prompted when Charles fell silent.

"And on the last night, I went out for dinner. Nothing fancy, just a steakhouse near the hotel. She was there, sitting alone at the bar, and she was..." He struggled for words. "Have you ever seen something so beautiful it actually hurt to look at? That's what she was like. Not just physically, though that was part of it. She had this... presence, this gravity that pulled everything toward her."

Alexis felt a chill crawl up her spine. "Go on."

"We talked. Or rather, she asked questions and I found myself answering them, telling her things I'd never told anyone. About my family history, about the construction business, about Elizabeth and our wedding plans. She seemed particularly interested in my genealogy, kept asking about my grandparents and great-grandparents, like she was tracing bloodlines."

"Why?" Katy asked from the doorway.

Charles shrugged helplessly. "She said my family carried traces of something ancient. Something that would make our union... significant. I didn't understand what she meant then. I'm not sure I understand it now."

"But you slept with her," Alexis said flatly.

Red crept up Charles's neck. "I was weak. She was... compelling in ways I can't explain. It was like she reached into my head and turned off every rational thought I'd ever had. Afterward, I felt sick with guilt. I loved Elizabeth, was planning to marry her in two weeks, and I'd just—" He buried his face in his hands.

"Did you tell Mom?" Alexis asked.

"I tried. God help me, I tried. But every time I opened my mouth to confess, the words wouldn't come. It was like something was stopping me from speaking."

The implications of that statement hung in the air like smoke. Alexis filed the detail away for later examination and pressed forward. "What happened next?"

"I flew home the next morning, threw myself into wedding preparations, tried to pretend it never happened. Elizabeth and I were married on schedule, went to Bermuda for our honeymoon." His voice grew distant, lost in memories that had probably haunted him for eighteen years. "That's when she came back."

"In Bermuda?" Alexis' mind was reaching out for any additional details that he may not have been sharing but her internal questioning resulted in the same details as his story.

"On the beach behind our hotel. Elizabeth had gone up to the room to shower, and I was sitting on the sand, watching the sunset, when she just... appeared. One moment the beach was empty, the next she was standing there like she'd stepped out of the shadows themselves."

Alexis's breath caught. The description matched what Pitts had done at the viewing—that uncanny ability to appear and disappear without warning. "What did she want?"

"To give me a gift." Charles's laugh held no humor. "That's what she called it. A gift for both Elizabeth and me. She told me she was pregnant, that the child was mine, but that she couldn't raise it in her world. Too dangerous, she said. Too many enemies who would use an innocent child as a weapon."

"So, she what, just handed me over?" Anger built in Alexis's chest, hot and bitter.

"Not exactly." Charles met her eyes for the first time since the conversation began. "She did something I still don't understand. Touched Elizabeth's stomach while she was sleeping and... transferred you somehow. Elizabeth woke up the next morning pregnant, with memories of conception that never actually happened. Nine months later, you were born, and neither of us questioned how or why."

The room fell silent except for the tick of the grandfather clock in the hallway. Alexis tried to process the impossibility of what her father was describing, but her rational mind recoiled from the implications. Transferred. Like she was some kind of mystical pregnancy that could be moved from one woman to another.

"That's impossible," she said finally.

"I thought so too. But then you started showing signs that you weren't entirely normal. The perfect memory, the way you needed almost no sleep, the strange dreams you'd have about places that didn't exist. And as you got older, there were other things. Lights flickering when you were upset. Electronics malfunctioning around you. The way animals seemed drawn to you, like they recognized something in you that humans couldn't see."

Alexis thought about Xander, the great horned owl who had made her rooftop perch part of his territory. About the way dogs always gravitated toward her at the park, their owners apologizing for their pets' unusual behavior. About the chronic problems with her cell phone and laptop that repair shops could never quite fix.

"Why didn't you tell me?"

"What was I supposed to say? That your real mother was some kind of supernatural being who could manipulate pregnancy like moving furniture? That you might be half-human?" Charles leaned forward, his expression desperate. "I wanted you to have a normal childhood, a normal life. I thought maybe if we just ignored the strangeness, it would go away."

"Well, it didn't." The words came out harsher than she'd intended. "It just got stronger. And now there are people who know what I am, people who want to use me for something, and I have no idea how to protect myself or anyone else."

"There's more," Charles said quietly.

"More what?"

"Your real mother, before she left that night in Bermuda, she gave me instructions. Rules to follow if anyone ever came looking for you. She said there would be signs when you were ready to learn the truth, and that when the time came, I should never keep you from her."

Alexis felt the world tilt sideways. "What does that mean, never keep me from her?"

"I think it means she's coming back."

The temperature in the room seemed to drop ten degrees. Outside, a car backfired, but the sound was muffled and distant, as if the house existed in a bubble separate from the rest of the world.

"How do you know?" Jamie asked.

Charles pointed toward the window, where darkness pressed against the glass like a living thing. "Because every night since Elizabeth died, I've felt her watching. Not that stranger you mentioned from today—something else. Something vast and patient and utterly alien. It's waiting for Alexis to be ready, and I think time is running out."

As if summoned by his words, the lights in the room began to flicker. Not the random electrical fluctuations Alexis had grown used to, but a deliberate pattern, like some kind of signal. The air grew heavy, charged with potential, and she felt something stirring in the depths of her chest, something that had been sleeping and was now beginning to wake.

"Dad," she whispered, but the word was lost as power surged through her like lightning, burning away the last of her numbness and leaving her raw and exposed and utterly transformed.

The room exploded into light.

When her vision cleared, Alexis found herself standing in the center of her bedroom, her very skin glowing with ethereal light and her hair crackling with residual energy. She caught a glimpse of herself in the floor-length mirror on the back of her door. The glow of her skin was fading and her eyes... Her eyes were not her own. Instead, glaring back at her were two pools of deepest black with what looked like flecks of starlight in them. It was too much. Alexis felt the world spin as she passed out in the blackness of dreams.

Alexis stood in front of two huge doors, each at least a dozen feet tall. She ran her fingers over the matte black surface thinking that they felt like stone of some sort, perhaps obsidian. She found it strange that they were so smooth but not even shiny enough for her to see her own reflection. They were icy to the touch, yet she felt comfortable, not cold.

Looking around, she could not make out any further details as to where she might be. It could have been a castle hallway or a cave for all she knew. She had taken a step away from the grand doors when there was a slight whisper of air. Turning around, she saw that the doors had begun to swing open just enough that she could walk through. Without hesitation, Alexis moved into the room. Even as every alarm bell in her head was blaring and screaming.

Within, there were no decorations or windows. The room was as black as ebony, just as the outside had been. She felt the air pressure change as the doors closed behind her. She sprinted at them. There was no handle, there wasn't even a seam that she could make out. Wherever she was, she was trapped.

In the span of a breath, the hard surface of the floor faded away, making it appear as though she was suspended in midair. She saw stars. At first, she thought it was from lack of oxygen; however, she soon understood that these were real stars she was seeing. Somehow, she was floating in the depths of space, as if it were the very substance from which the chamber was made.

Her fine blonde hair floated in the lack of atmosphere and Alexis wondered how she could be alive without air to breathe. She manipulated her body to turn in circles, attempting to grasp any reference to her possible location or a star formation that she might recognize. In the distance, she saw an approaching figure. It was so strange to see that it was discernible against the blackness of space, as if it were the very essence of the absence of light.

Flowing ebony in the approximate shape of a person moved back and forth across her field of vision. She was unable to judge the distance to the figure but knew that it was real. Someone else was out here with her. Like a streak of black lightning, the figure raced toward her, wrapping itself around her, enveloping her but never quite coming into physical contact.

Alexis strained to make out a face or visage of some type to no avail. It was like the darkness itself had come alive and was moving with her, holding her, but not confining her. She couldn't help but feel out of sorts, confused and frustrated. Was this real? What was happening to her?

A sea of faces flickered into view as Alexis managed to open her eyes. Charles, Katy, and Keats sat beside her on the floor of her bedroom, their eyes wide with shock and something that might have been awe. Only Katy moved, leaning forward with the calm efficiency of someone who had seen impossible things before.

"Well," she said, her voice steady despite the supernatural fireworks that had just lit up the living room. "I suppose there's no hiding it anymore."

"What? What happened?" Alexis' words were clearer than her thoughts.

"You just fucking teleported!" Keats exclaimed, unable to contain his excitement.

"Jameson!" his mother reprimanded. "Language!" Keats just smiled and shrugged.

"I… I what?"

"One second you are lit up like a Christmas tree and the next, POOF!, you were gone. We heard you hit the floor from downstairs and rushed up here. How are you feeling?"

Alexis stared at her hands, watching glow dissipate like fading starlight at dawn. The power was still there, humming beneath her skin, waiting for direction. For the first time in her life, she felt complete, like she'd been walking around with a missing piece of herself and had finally found it.

The feeling should have been terrifying. Instead, it felt like coming home.

"What am I?" she asked, though she wasn't sure if she was addressing the room or the universe itself.

The answer came not in words but in images that flooded her mind—vast cosmic spaces where night reigned eternal, ancient beings who had existed since the dawn of time, power that could reshape reality with a thought. And underneath it all, a voice she had been hearing in dreams for as long as she could remember, singing to her before she could even crawl, calling her home to a destiny she was finally ready to embrace.

Daughter, the voice whispered, and Alexis felt tears on her cheeks for the first time since Elizabeth died. Not tears of grief, but of recognition.

She was no longer the lost girl who couldn't cry at her mother's funeral.

She was something far more dangerous.

And somewhere in the darkness beyond the windows, ancient powers were stirring, drawn by the awakening of one who carried their blood in her veins.

CHAPTER 4: FIRST STEPS

The next morning arrived with the kind of aggressive brightness that made Alexis feel like the sun was personally offended by her existence. She stood at her bedroom window, watching Charles load cardboard boxes into the back of his pickup truck with the methodical precision of a man who had decided that staying busy was the only thing preventing complete emotional collapse.

She had a million more questions than she did yesterday. The fact that she literally teleported from one physical space to another seemed impossible. Hell. It *was* impossible by all known standards.

Her phone buzzed against the nightstand. Another text from Jamie: *You okay? Haven't heard from you since last night.*

She wasn't okay. Nothing about discovering you were half-supernatural qualified as okay. But admitting that felt like giving up, and Alexis Rain had never been particularly good at surrendering.

Instead of answering the text, she pulled on jeans and a T-shirt and headed downstairs to find Charles sitting at the kitchen table with a cup of coffee that had gone cold an hour ago. He looked up when she entered, and she saw her own exhaustion reflected in his bloodshot eyes.

"Graduation's tonight," he said without preamble. As if last night never even happened.

"I know."

"Your mother would have wanted—"

"Dad." She cut him off before he could finish the thought. "After everything that happened last night, you really think we should be worried about walking across a stage in polyester robes?"

"I think we should be worried about maintaining some semblance of normalcy while we figure out what comes next." His voice carried the kind of forced authoritative calm that came from years of managing construction crews and temperamental clients. "Besides, graduation isn't just about you. It's about the people who love you getting to see you take your first steps into adulthood."

The irony wasn't lost on her. Her first steps into adulthood had apparently involved manifesting supernatural powers that could level a room. But Charles was right about one thing—if there were people watching her now, people like Pitts who were interested in her abilities, then maintaining normal appearances might be the only thing keeping them safe.

"Fine," she said. "But after tonight, we need to start getting real answers. I can't keep pretending everything's normal when I'm apparently some kind of cosmic anomaly."

Charles nodded, relief evident in the way his shoulders relaxed. "Agreed. But one thing at a time."

Several hours later, Alexis found herself sitting in the passenger seat of Keats's Honda Civic, watching Mount Pleasant High School's parking lot fill with families armed with cameras and flowers. The sight should have been comforting—a return to the predictable rhythms of teenage life—but instead it felt like observing an alien ritual from the outside.

"You sure you're up for this?" Keats asked, following her gaze toward the gymnasium where graduation would take place. "Because you look like someone who spent the night wrestling with existential crises."

"Close enough." She turned to study his profile, noting the way his jaw tightened whenever he was worried. She peered directly into his green eyes. "How are you handling all this? The supernatural weirdness, I mean. Most people would be running for the hills by now."

"Most people didn't spend twelve years being best friends with someone who could remember every conversation they'd ever had and needed two hours of sleep a night." He grinned, but there was something forced about the expression. "Besides, someone's got to keep you from accidentally destroying the world with your newfound cosmic powers."

"That's assuming I *can* control them."

"You will." His confidence was absolute, unshakeable. "You've never met a challenge you couldn't master through sheer stubborn determination. Supernatural abilities can't be that different from calculus or martial arts."

She wanted to believe him, but the memory of silver light exploding from her skin like a solar flare suggested that some challenges might be bigger than determination could handle. Still, his faith in her was anchoring, a reminder that not everything had changed overnight.

"Keats," she said as they climbed out of the car. "Last night, when I lost control… Were you scared?"

He considered the question seriously, the way he always did when she asked him something important. "Scared? No. Impressed? Absolutely. You should've seen yourself, Al. You looked like you were channeling starlight, itself. And then… That whole teleporting thing. Holy Star Trek, Batman!"

"And that doesn't worry you?"

"Should it?" He stopped walking and turned to face her fully. "You're still you. You're still the girl who won't eat pizza with pineapple and corrects people's grammar even when they're not asking for help. The fact that you can apparently bend reality doesn't change the important stuff."

Before she could respond, a familiar voice called out across the parking lot. "Alexis! Jamie! Over here!"

They turned to see Mrs. Patterson from AP English waving at them from the gymnasium entrance, her arms loaded with programs and corsages. Behind her, a steady stream of seniors in cap and gown moved toward the building like a river of royal blue polyester.

"Showtime," Jamie murmured, but he said it with a smile.

The next two hours passed in a blur of speeches and applause and names being called in alphabetical order. Alexis sat in the front row between Jamie and Rebecca Sanchez, trying to focus on Principal Davidson's remarks about bright futures and limitless potential while her mind churned through everything that had happened since Elizabeth's death.

When her name was called, she walked across the stage on autopilot, shook hands with people whose faces she would remember forever but whose words disappeared into the white noise of her racing thoughts. The diploma felt thin and insubstantial in her hands, a piece of paper that was supposed to represent the culmination of twelve years of education but felt more like a participation trophy.

From the audience, Charles applauded with the kind of fierce pride that made her chest tighten. Beside him, Katy dabbed at her eyes with a tissue, playing the role of surrogate mother with the same dedication Elizabeth would have brought to the moment.

Elizabeth should be here, Alexis thought, and for the first time the grief hit her with full force. Not the numb acceptance that had carried her through the past few days, but a raw, violent sense of loss that made breathing difficult.

Her mother had planned for this moment. Had bought the dress that had hung in Alexis's closet, had made reservations at Alexis's favorite restaurant for the celebration dinner they would never have. Had died on a mountain road before she could see her daughter graduate.

The unfairness of it burned through Alexis like acid, and she felt power stirring in response to her emotional state. The air around her began to shimmer, and she gritted her teeth against the urge to let that power loose, to channel her grief into something that could remake the world according to her will.

Control, she told herself. Not here. Not now.

By the time the ceremony ended, and families began gathering for photos, Alexis had managed to lock her abilities down to a low simmer. But the effort left her feeling hollow, like she'd spent the past two hours holding her breath.

"Pictures?" Charles asked as they met up outside the gymnasium.

"Sure." She submitted to the ritual, standing with Jamie and various classmates while parents and siblings documented the moment for posterity. But her attention kept drifting to the crowd, searching for faces that didn't belong, for signs that she was being watched.

She found nothing obviously threatening, but the paranoia remained. Pitts had found her at Elizabeth's viewing with no apparent difficulty. Who was to say he or others like him weren't here now, cataloging her reactions, planning their next move?

"Earth to Alexis," Jamie said, appearing at her elbow with two bottles of water. "You look like you're about to vibrate out of your skin."

"Just thinking."

"About?"

"About how we go from here to figuring out what I really am without getting everyone we care about killed in the process."

The question hung between them like a loaded weapon. Around them, families celebrated and took pictures and made plans for the future, blissfully unaware that supernatural forces were moving in the shadows of their ordinary world.

"One step at a time," Jamie said finally. "Starting with research. You said Pitts mentioned your real mother being something more than human. Maybe there are records, legends, something that can tell us what we're dealing with."

"And how exactly do we research supernatural beings? Check out library books on 'So You Think Your Daughter is Part Deity'?" Keats chuckled aloud at that.

"We could start with your perfect memory." His expression grew thoughtful. "You said last night that power felt familiar, like you'd been suppressing it your whole life. What if there are other things you know but don't know you know? Information that's been locked away in your subconscious?"

The suggestion sent a chill through her. If Jamie was right, if her abilities included access to knowledge she wasn't aware of possessing, then the answers they needed might already be inside her head. The question was how to access them without losing control again.

"We should go home," she said. "Start experimenting. See what I can dig up."

"Agreed. But carefully." Jamie's expression grew serious. "Whatever happened last night was powerful enough to leave scorch marks. If you tap into something bigger—"

"I'll be careful." She touched his arm, feeling the warmth of human contact like an anchor to normalcy. "I promise."

But even as she made the promise, Alexis felt the power stirring beneath her skin like a caged animal testing the strength of its bars. Whatever was awakening inside her was vast and ancient and not entirely under her control.

The question wasn't whether she would tap into something bigger.

The question was whether she would survive it when she did.

As they walked toward the parking lot, Charles fell into step beside them. "I'm proud of you," he said quietly. "Both of you. Your mother would be too."

"Thanks, Dad." But as she said it, Alexis found herself wondering if Elizabeth really would be proud, or if she'd be terrified by what her daughter was becoming.

The thought followed her home, a dark whisper that suggested the hardest part wasn't behind them.

It was just beginning.

Three hours later, Alexis sat cross-legged on her bedroom floor with Keats staring at her as if looking at an insect under a microscope. He'd been asking her a bunch of ridiculous questions about the capitol's of foreign countries and why certain beans and leaves contained caffeine. She was pretty shocked to learn (from her own mind) that plants produce caffeine as a natural defense mechanism - it's essentially a pesticide they manufacture to protect themselves from threats. Pretty cool, if you think about it.

"Stop it," she said. "You're being creepy."

"Sorry. You ready?"

Charles had just returned the rental chairs from the reception and joined them for Keats' testing. The young man had laid it out. There was only one way to figure this out and that was to use the scientific approach and verify, verify, verify.

Her father sat in the reading chair by the window, nursing his mug of coffee and watching the proceedings with the careful attention of someone who wasn't sure whether to be proud or terrified.

"Okay," Keats said, pulling out his phone and opening what appeared to be a notes app. "Let's establish some parameters first. You said you've always had perfect recall of everything you've read, seen, or heard, right?"

"Right." Alexis tucked her legs under her on the bed, still feeling oddly disconnected from her own body after last night's teleportation incident. The black had faded from her eyes, returning them to their normal blue pretty quickly, but she kept catching herself touching her face as if to confirm she was still herself.

"But based on what just happened with the questions about Bhutan and caffeine, it seems like you can access information you've never encountered before." Keats's green eyes were bright with scientific curiosity. "So, the question is: are there limits? Can you access any knowledge that exists, or only certain types?"

"Only one way to find out," Alexis said, though the prospect both excited and unsettled her. If she really could tap into all human knowledge, what did that make her? And more importantly, why?

"Let's start with something completely random." Keats scrolled through his phone. "What's the melting point of tungsten?"

"3,695 degrees Kelvin. Or 3,422 degrees Celsius." The answer came as naturally as if he'd asked her favorite color. "It has the highest melting point of any element."

"Okay, that could still be something you read somewhere and forgot you read."

Keats made a note. "How about... what's the current population of Ulaanbaatar, Mongolia?"

Alexis paused, feeling an odd sensation like reaching into a vast library that existed somewhere beyond her physical mind. "Approximately 1.4 million people as of 2023. Though the exact number fluctuates with seasonal migration patterns."

"I don't think that's something that would be in any textbook you've studied," Charles said quietly.

"No kidding," Alexis agreed, a little disturbed by how easily the information had come to her. "Keats, what are you writing down?"

"Everything. We need to understand the scope of this." He looked up at her with the expression he got when working through complex physics problems. "Try this one: what's the recipe for Coca-Cola?"

"That's not known," Alexis said immediately. "The formula is a trade secret held by the Coca-Cola Company. Only a few people in the world have access to the complete recipe, and it's stored in a vault at the World of Coca-Cola Museum in Atlanta."

"Interesting," Keats murmured. "So, you can't access information that's deliberately kept secret. Unless... "

"Unless what, hotshot?" She crossed her arms over her chest and gave him that withering look that screamed her impatience with him.

"Focus on the few people who do know the recipe. Can you retrieve it from them, from *their* knowledge?"

"Apparently not."

"Try."

She closed her eyes, setting her current frustration aside. She searched first for information that would point to the actual people who did have access to the exact recipe. Within seconds, she had several names. After a few more queries, she found the recipe. One the guardians of the secret recipe weren't so good at keeping secrets after all. He'd bragged about knowing it to his wife. He even proved it by having his own hand-written copy. In another few seconds, the secret was revealed in her mid and she had it.

"Oh, crap," she said, opening her eyes. Keats and Charles stared at her. "I know the recipe."

"Interesting." Keats was in full science mode. "What about classified government information? Like... what's the current nuclear launch code for the United States?"

"I have no idea," Alexis said, and felt oddly relieved. "That knowledge feels... blocked, somehow. Like it's behind a wall I can't get over or through."

"Good," Charles said firmly. "The last thing we need is for you to accidentally access state secrets."

Keats grinned. "Though it would make our history tests a lot more interesting." His expression grew more serious. "Let's try something historical but obscure. What did Napoleon eat for breakfast on the morning of the Battle of Waterloo?"

Alexis concentrated, reaching for that strange mental library again. "Bread, coffee, and a small piece of cheese. He complained to his valet that the coffee was too bitter." She blinked. "How could I possibly know that?"

"Because someone, somewhere, recorded it," Keats said, making another note. "Maybe a historian found it in a diary, or a servant's memoir, or military records. The information *exists* in human knowledge, so you can access it."

"But that seems impossible. How could my mind connect to information I've never encountered?"

"I don't know. But let's test the limits." Keats was fully in his element now, the way he got when presented with a puzzle that required both logic and creativity. "What about something more recent? What did I have for lunch yesterday?"

"A turkey sandwich with mustard, no mayo, and a bag of those barbecue chips you're always eating. You also had an apple, but you didn't finish it because it was mealy." Alexis paused. "Wait, that's just observational memory. I saw you eating lunch."

"True. But what about this: what was my first word as a baby?"

"Cookie," Alexis said without hesitation, then froze. "Oh my God. How did I know that?"

Keats stared at her. "That's... that's actually right. Mom told me about it when I was ten. I demanded cookies for breakfast and when she said no, I pointed at the cabinet and yelled 'cookie' until she gave in."

"But I wasn't there when you were a baby," Alexis said, a chill running down her spine. "And you never told me that story."

"No, but the information exists," Charles said slowly. "Your friend's mother knows it. Maybe she shared it with a friend," he glanced over at Keats, "Because it's just so damned cute." Keats grimaced. "Or maybe other family members were there when it happened."

"So, I can access any knowledge that any human being possesses?" The implications were staggering.

"Let's find out," Keats said. "Something even more personal. What's my middle name?"

"Michael," Alexis replied automatically. "Jameson Michael Keats, named after your grandfather on your mother's side."

"And my grandfather's middle name?"

"Patrick. Michael Patrick Keats." She looked at him in confusion. "But I've never met your grandfather, and you've never mentioned his full name."

"Because I didn't know it myself until last month when Mom was filling out some insurance forms," Keats said softly. "She mentioned it in passing. Al, you're accessing information about me that I barely know myself."

The weight of what she was capable of began to settle on Alexis's shoulders. If she could tap into any knowledge possessed by any human being, the applications were limitless—and terrifying.

"Try something really obscure," she said. "Something that maybe only one or two people in the world would know."

Keats thought for a moment. "What's the real name of the person who designed the security system for the Louvre?"

"Jean-Claude Martineau," Alexis said, then caught herself. "But that could be public record somewhere."

"What about his daughter's favorite stuffed animal when she was five?"

"A purple elephant named Gaston." The information came as clearly as everything else. "She took it everywhere until she was seven, when she lost it at a beach in Nice."

"Jesus," Keats breathed. "That's not public record. That's family memory."

"This is getting scary," Alexis said. "What if I can access anything anyone has ever known? What about private thoughts, secrets people have never told anyone?"

"Let's test that," Keats said, his scientific curiosity overriding any concern about privacy. "What am I thinking right now?"

Alexis concentrated, reaching out with that strange mental faculty. "I... nothing. I can't read your mind."

"What about something I know but have never told anyone?"

"Like what?"

"Just try. Focus on me and see if you can access something I've never shared."

Alexis closed her eyes and extended her consciousness toward her best friend. For a moment, she felt the edge of something—a memory, a piece of knowledge that belonged to him alone. But it was hazy, indistinct, like trying to see through frosted glass.

"There's something about... a dream? Something that scared you when you were twelve?" She opened her eyes. "But I can't see it clearly. It feels protected somehow."

Keats had gone very still. "What kind of dream?"

"I don't know. It's like there's a barrier around it." Alexis studied his face, noting the subtle tension that had crept into his posture. "What is it? What did you dream about?"

"Nothing important," he said, but his voice carried a note she'd never heard before—carefully controlled, as if he were weighing every word. "Just kid stuff."

There was something he wasn't telling her, but before Alexis could pursue it further, her father spoke up.

"Maybe we should take a break," Charles said. "This is a lot to process, and it's been a long day."

"Actually, I want to try one more thing," Keats said, though he still looked unsettled. "Something completely different. Al, you've always been incredible at martial arts, right? Perfect form, amazing reflexes?"

"I've had good training," Alexis said modestly.

"But what if it's more than that? What if you don't just have access to all human knowledge, but to all human skill?" Keats was leaning forward now, his earlier discomfort forgotten in favor of a new theory. "Think about it. Every martial arts technique that's ever been developed, every form that's ever been perfected. What if you can access all of that?"

"That's... that's not how muscle memory works," Alexis protested. "You can't just download physical abilities."

"Can't you? You just accessed memories that aren't yours, knowledge you've never learned. Why not skills too?"

Before Alexis could respond, Keats was moving. He came at her with a combination she'd never seen him use—a fluid series of strikes that looked like they belonged to a completely different martial art than what they practiced at the dojo.

Without thinking, Alexis responded. Her body moved on its own, executing a perfect counter that seemed to come from some deep well of knowledge she hadn't known she possessed. She caught his wrist, redirected his momentum, and suddenly Keats was sitting on the floor looking stunned.

"Where did that come from?" he asked.

"I have no idea," Alexis said, staring at her own hands. "It felt like... like I was remembering something I'd never learned."

"Wing Chun," Charles said quietly. "That was a Wing Chun technique. But you've never studied that style."

"No, but someone has," Keats said, picking himself up off the floor. "And apparently Al can access their knowledge of it."

The three of them sat in silence for a moment, absorbing the implications. Alexis felt like she was standing at the edge of an ocean whose depths she couldn't fathom. The abilities she was discovering went far beyond anything she'd imagined possible.

"Keats," she said slowly, "how did you know to try that combination? I've never seen you move like that before."

He grinned that damned I'm-so-proud-of-myself grin. "I saw it on Kung-fu theater a few weeks ago. I don't know. It just felt right in the moment."

"But you executed it perfectly. Like you'd been trained in that style."

"Lucky guess?" But the way he said it suggested he didn't believe his own explanation.

Alexis studied her best friend's face, noting details her enhanced awareness was cataloging automatically. The way his eyes had briefly unfocused when he'd launched his attack, as if he were accessing information from somewhere else. The unconscious certainty in his movements that suggested training he'd never received. The fact that he'd known exactly what questions to ask to test her abilities, as if some part of him had always suspected what she was capable of.

"Keats," she said carefully, "is there something you're not telling me?"

"Al, you just discovered you can access the entire sum of human knowledge and skill. Maybe we should focus on that instead of psychoanalyzing my lucky guess."

There was definitely something he wasn't sharing, but Alexis could see in his expression that he wasn't ready to talk about it. Whatever his secret was, it would have to wait. She had bigger mysteries to unravel.

"So, what does this mean?" she asked. "What am I?" She looked at her father.

"I don't know," Charles said. "But your birth mother said this day would come. When you'd begin to understand your true nature."

"Did she say anything else? Anything that might help us figure out what's happening to me?"

Charles was quiet for a long moment. "She said you were more than human, but not less. That you would bridge worlds in ways that had never been done before." He looked at her with eyes full of love and concern. "She also said there would be those who would try to use you, and those who would try to destroy you."

A thought occurred to Alexis, something that made her sit up straighter. "What if I can find out who she is? If I can access all human knowledge, maybe someone, somewhere, has recorded information about her."

"How would you even begin to look?" Keats asked.

"By finding someone who studies things like this. Someone who might have encountered others like me." Alexis closed her eyes and reached out with her new abilities, searching for information about people who researched the supernatural, the impossible, the spaces where myth and reality intersected.

The answer came almost immediately, along with a wealth of supporting information that flowed through her mind like water.

"A name. Dr. Marcus Hough, Columbia University. He's an expert on exactly the kind of things we're dealing with." She stood up, brushing dust from her jeans. "I'm going to see him."

"When?"

"Now."

Keats nearly choked on his own breath. "Now? As in, right now? Al, it's almost eight o'clock on a Friday night. And Columbia is a ten-hour drive from here."

"Not if I teleport." She stood to move toward the door. The thought of teleporting again freaked her out more than a little. Both Charles' and Keats' reactions only increased that feeling.

"Whoa! Wait just a minute there, young lady," Charles said.

"This is insane." Keats set down his cup of coffee and stepped into her path. "You can't just beam yourself off to New York because a name popped into your head."

"Why not?"

"Because—" He struggled for words. "Because normal people can't teleport. Because normal people don't get mystical downloads of information about college professors. Because you just manifested supernatural powers twenty-four hours ago and probably shouldn't be making major decisions while you're still adjusting."

The concern in his voice was genuine, and under normal circumstances she might have listened to it. But these weren't normal circumstances, and every instinct she possessed was screaming that time was running out.

"I can do this," she said. She stared at the both of them, the determination at finding the truth about herself was clouding her judgment. Even she realized that. Yet, she couldn't stop herself. "This is important. I can feel it."

"Feel it how?" Keats stared daggers at his best friend's lack of forethought and recklessness.

She paused, trying to put the sensation into words. It was like having an itch she couldn't scratch, a certainty that the answers she needed were waiting just beyond her reach. "It's hard to explain. Ever since last night, it's like there's something guiding me, pointing me in the right direction. And every time I think about Dr. Hough, that feeling gets stronger."

"Or," Keats said carefully, "something is manipulating you into making reckless decisions. You said Pitts was interested in recruiting you. What if this sudden urge to seek out experts is part of his plan?"

The possibility stopped her cold. She hadn't considered that her newfound access to information might be compromised, that someone else might be feeding her thoughts disguised as intuition. But even as the doubt crept in, the certainty about Hough remained unshaken.

"I have to take the risk," she said finally. "We need answers and sitting here wondering what's real isn't going to get them."

"Then we go together."

"Keats—"

"Together," he said, and looked over meaningfully at Charles. Alexis' father seemed to ponder the situation thoroughly before nodding. Keats looked back to Alexis. "Together," he reiterated.

CHAPTER 5: DIVINE INTERVENTION

Alexis wanted to argue, but the relief that flooded through her at his offer told her everything she needed to know. She didn't want to do this alone. She was just scared of putting him in danger.

"Fine," she said. "But if things get weird..."

"Weirder than they already are?" He grinned. "I think that ship has sailed."

Alexis spent the following morning practicing the strange teleportation ability she'd gained. The more she tried and succeeded at jumping from one location to another, the more she realized it wasn't really teleportation. It was more like she was stepping into the ether of the universe and stepping out wherever her mind dictated. After several hours of getting a handle on the ability, she was exhausted and lay down for a nap while Keats and Charles likely went over the logistics.

A few hours later, just after noon, Alexis and Keats stood in her living room about to jaunt off into the unknown. She had gotten to practice with Keats a few times and they realized that she had to be touching him for him to be able to move with her through the ether. He wasn't a fan but handled it with a self-possession that was Keats' mainstay.

"All right," she said. She gave her dad a quick hug. "We'll be fine, Dad. I promise."

"You better." He glanced pointedly at Keats. "Take care of her."

"More likely the other way around," he replied with his usual snark. He noted the expression on Charles' expression reeled his snark back in quickly. "Yes sir," he added.

"Ready?" she said. Keats nodded. She took his hand and they both stepped forward, disappearing into the ether, leaving Charles to wonder at this God-awful situation and praying that his daughter would be okay.

Dr. Marcus Hough lived in a brownstone on the Upper West Side that looked like it had been decorated by someone with a serious book addiction and no interest in interior design. Towering shelves lined every wall, packed with volumes in languages Alexis couldn't identify. The air smelled of old paper and something that might have been incense.

Hough himself was younger than she'd expected, maybe forty, with prematurely gray hair and the kind of pale complexion that came from spending too much time indoors. He answered the door in jeans and a Columbia sweatshirt, looking more like a graduate student than a tenured professor.

"Dr. Hough?" Alexis extended her hand. "I'm Alexis Rain. This is my friend Jamie Keats. I called earlier about needing some research assistance."

"Of course." His handshake was firm but brief, and she noticed the way his eyes catalogued details about her appearance with academic precision. "Please, come in. Can I offer you coffee? Tea?"

"Coffee would be great," Keats said, settling into a leather armchair that looked older than both of them combined.

Hough disappeared into the kitchen, leaving them alone among the towers of books. Alexis ran her fingers along the spines, noting titles on subjects ranging from ancient astronomy to modern chaos theory. Whatever else Dr. Hough might be, he was clearly serious about his research.

"So," he said, returning with a tray of steaming mugs. "You mentioned on the phone that you were researching primordial deities for a family genealogy project. That's a rather unusual approach to family history."

"It's a rather unusual family," Alexis replied, accepting a mug that warmed her hands. "I recently learned that my biological mother might have some connection to ancient Greek mythology. Something to do with that, anyway."

The change in Hough's demeanor was immediate and dramatic. The casual friendliness evaporated, replaced by sharp attention that made Alexis feel like a specimen under a microscope.

He set down his mug with careful precision. "Your mother... and mythology?" Hough leaned back, fingers drumming against his coffee mug. "That's not usually how genealogy research works." Alexis shifted in her chair. How much could she tell him? "Have you ever felt like you don't quite... fit? Like there's something wrong with you that you can't name?" "Everyone feels that way sometimes." "Not like this." She stared at her hands. "I remember everything. Every conversation, every book, every moment since I was three. I sleep maybe two hours a night. And lately..." She trailed off, watching shadows seem to reach toward her across the floor. Hough's expression sharpened. "Lately?"

"Lately, some manifestations that could be described as... unusual."

Hough leaned forward, his academic detachment giving way to something hungrier. "What kind of manifestations?"

"The kind that leave marks and make electronics malfunction." She met his gaze steadily. "Professor, I need to know what I'm dealing with. If my heritage is really connected with what most believe to be fairy tales, what does that make me?"

"Assuming your suspicions are correct?" Hough stood and began pacing, his movements sharp and agitated. "It would make you what we call a Scion. A half-blood. The child of a deity and a mortal. In other words, a demigod."

"Demigods are real?"

"Oh, yes. Though most don't survive to adulthood." His voice carried a clinical detachment that made Alexis's skin crawl. "The divine and mortal natures are fundamentally incompatible. The strain typically manifests as madness, usually around puberty. Those who don't break mentally often die from the physical stress of containing power their bodies weren't designed to handle."

"But some survive?"

"A few. The stable ones are extraordinarily rare and extraordinarily dangerous." He stopped pacing and fixed her with a stare that felt like being dissected. "From what you've described—and it isn't much to go on—I'd suspect you may be the daughter of Nyx." He hesitated. "Which would be problematic, at best."

"Why?" Her curiosity was getting the best of her. Nyx? Her real mother?

"If you really are Nyx's daughter, you would be the first of her bloodline in recorded history. Nyx has never taken mortal lovers, never shown interest in the human world. She's too ancient, too powerful, too removed from earthly concerns."

"Maybe she had a reason this time," Keats suggested.

Hough's laugh held no humor. "Primordial deities don't have reasons in the way humans understand them. They have imperatives, cosmic functions they exist to fulfill. If Nyx broke her pattern of isolation to create a Scion, it's because something fundamental about the universal order has changed."

The implications of that statement settled over the room like a shroud. Alexis felt the weight of cosmic significance pressing down on her, transforming her from a confused teenager into some kind of pivotal figure in forces she couldn't begin to comprehend.

"What would she want with a daughter?" she asked quietly.

"Unknown. But I can tell you where to find someone who might have answers." Hough moved to his desk and pulled out a leather-bound address book. "Rose Hartford. She's housed at St. Anne's Care Facility in London. Daughter of Athena, goddess of wisdom and strategy. She was brilliant once—child prodigy, early admission to Oxford, doctorate in theoretical physics by age sixteen. Then the madness took her."

"And you think she can help me?"

"If anyone can provide insight into divine parentage and its consequences, it would be her. During her lucid moments, she demonstrates knowledge that goes far beyond anything she could have learned through conventional means." He scribbled an address on a piece of paper and handed it to her. "But be warned—even stable Scions attract attention. There are forces that view your kind as either valuable assets or dangerous threats. By seeking answers, you risk exposing yourself to both."

Alexis tucked the address into her pocket, filing away the warning along with everything else Hough had told her. The conversation had answered some questions while raising dozens of others, but at least now she had a direction to move in.

"Thank you," she said, standing to leave. "You've been incredibly helpful."

"Wait." Hough's voice stopped her at the door. "There's something else you should know. The fact that you're stable, that you've survived this long without breaking—it means you're not just any Scion. You're something special, even by their standards. That kind of rarity tends to attract the wrong kind of attention."

"What kind of attention?"

"The kind that gets people killed."

Outside on the sidewalk, Keats waited until they were out of earshot before speaking. "Well, that was ominous."

"But informative." Alexis pulled out her phone and started searching for flights to London. "We need to see Rose Hartford."

"Al, maybe we should slow down. Think about what Hough said about attracting attention."

"I am thinking about it. Which is why we need to move fast, before whoever's watching decides to make their next move." She pulled out her phone and found a red-eye flight with availability and started booking tickets. "Besides, what choice do I have? Ignore this and hope it goes away? Pretend I'm normal when I can apparently access information that doesn't exist and shoot lightning from my fingertips?"

"Point taken." Keats sighed. "London it is. But I'm driving you to the airport, and I'm coming with you."

"Keats—"

"Non-negotiable. We're in this together now, remember?"

As they walked toward the subway station, Alexis felt a familiar prickling sensation between her shoulder blades. She turned to scan the street behind them but saw nothing obviously threatening—just the usual urban mix of pedestrians and traffic.

Still, the feeling persisted, a certainty that they were being watched by eyes that had found them despite all their precautions.

The game was escalating, and she was no longer sure who was playing and who was being played.

But one thing was becoming clear: answers came with a price, and that price was rising with every step they took deeper into the supernatural world.

CHAPTER 6: NOT THAT SIMPLE

Alexis and Keats stepped from the ether onto College Street, not too far from home. She needed a minute to gather her thoughts. The walk gave her time to process everything the professor had told them. Scions. Half-bloods. Children of gods who usually died screaming or went insane before their sixteenth birthday. The weight of that knowledge sat in her chest like a stone, cold and heavy and impossible to ignore.

"You're thinking too loud," Keats said as they turned onto the tree-lined street that led to her house. "I can practically hear the gears grinding from here."

"Just trying to figure out what comes next." She kicked a loose stone, watching it skitter across the asphalt. "Hough gave us a lead, but London might as well be on Mars for all the good it does us right now."

"Why? We've got passports, we've got money…"

"We've got a father who's already lost his wife and will probably lock me in my room if I suggest flying to another continent to interview an insane woman about my divine heritage." The words came out sharper than she'd intended, frustration bleeding through her carefully maintained composure.

Keats stopped walking. "Then don't ask permission."

"What?"

"You heard me. Don't ask permission. You're eighteen, you're legally an adult, and you've got access to your trust fund as of graduation. Charles can't stop you from leaving."

The suggestion should have seemed outrageous, but instead it felt like a key turning in a lock she hadn't realized existed. For eighteen years, she'd lived within the boundaries other people had set for her—parents, teachers, and social expectations that treated her like a child despite the adult-level intelligence trapped in her teenage body. But those boundaries were illusions, weren't they? Lines drawn in sand that she could cross whenever she chose.

"He'll never forgive me," she said quietly.

"Maybe not. But he'd rather have a daughter who was alive and angry at him than a daughter who was dead because of mysterious strangers out to do her in." Keats's voice carried the kind of certainty that came from knowing someone better than they knew themselves. "Besides, you think he's going to be able to protect you from whatever's coming? From people like Pitts, who can make entire rooms of people freeze up with a thought?"

The memory of the viewing sent ice through her veins. Charles was a good man, a strong man, but he was also fundamentally human. Whatever was hunting her operated on a level that made human strength irrelevant.

"Even if I decide to go," she said, "London's still thousands of miles away. Even with your brilliant plan to bypass parental consent, that's a huge difference from a quick step to New York."

"Is it?"

Alexis stopped walking. "You think I can teleport that far?"

"I think you won't know until you try. And I think sitting around wondering about your abilities isn't nearly as useful as actually testing them." His expression grew serious. "Look, I know this is scary. I know it would be easier to pretend none of this is happening and go to college like normal teenagers. But you're not a normal teenager, and ignoring that fact isn't going to make it go away."

They'd reached her house, its familiar silhouette dark against the star-filled sky. No lights showed in the windows—Charles was either asleep or sitting in his workshop, where he went when he needed to think through problems too big for the kitchen table.

"Come on," Alexis said, leading Keats around to the backyard. "If I'm going to practice stepping through dimensions, I'd rather do it somewhere without breakable objects."

The backyard stretched away from the house in a sweep of lawn bordered by the old oak trees that had probably been there since before Mount Pleasant existed. Alexis had spent countless hours out here as a child, building forts and climbing trees and learning that the night held no terrors for her—only peace.

Now, standing under the canopy of stars, she tried to recapture that sense of belonging she'd always felt in darkness.

"I know you've been practicing and stepping to New York was pretty cool. But how does it work?" Keats asked, settling onto the porch steps to watch. "The stepping thing, I mean."

"I'm not sure." Alexis closed her eyes, trying to remember the sensation from the night she'd first manifested her abilities. "When it happened the first time, I wasn't trying to do anything. I was just... somewhere else suddenly."

"Try thinking about where you want to go. Like you did with New York. Only be more specific. Picture it in your mind."

She thought about her perch on the roof of the house. For a moment, nothing happened. Then the world around her began to shimmer, like heat waves rising from summer asphalt, and she felt something vast and welcoming reaching out to embrace her.

The ether.

That's what she called it—the space between spaces, the void that existed in the gaps between realities. She could feel it now, patient and infinite, waiting for her to step forward into its embrace.

But when she tried to move, nothing happened. Her feet remained firmly planted on the grass of her backyard, and after several long moments the shimmering faded.

"Anything?" Keats asked.

"Almost. I can feel it, but for some reason I can't seem to actually step into it." Frustration built in her chest. "It's like being able to see a door but not being able to open it. I don't understand. I mean, we just stepped from New York to North Carolina in the blink of an eye."

"Maybe you're trying too hard. When it happened before, you said you weren't thinking about it?"

"I was upset the first time. Then, for Hough's, I was pretty freaking determined. Angry about my life, secrets, just overwhelmed by everything." She thought back to that moment when her emotional control had shattered completely. "Maybe strong emotion is the trigger?"

"Then get emotional."

"It's not that simple."

"Isn't it?" Keats stood up, his expression challenging. "Your mother just died, your father lied to you for eighteen years, and some supernatural creep is stalking you because you're apparently the daughter of a primordial goddess. If that's not enough to generate strong emotion, I don't know what is."

The words hit their target with surgical precision. Grief, anger, and betrayal crashed through her like a tidal wave, sweeping away the careful control she had maintained since leaving Hough's office. Power built in her chest, silver light beginning to leak from her skin, and she felt the barriers between dimensions growing thin.

This time, when she stepped forward, the world fell away.

The ether was more open this time. Instead of empty void, it was filled with a soft, welcoming darkness that felt like coming home. She existed here as pure consciousness, unbound by the physical limitations of flesh and bone, aware of infinite pathways stretching in directions that had no names. Yet, she still held onto her physical form.

She could go anywhere from here. London, Tokyo, the surface of the moon. Distance was meaningless in a place that existed outside normal space-time. All she had to do was choose a destination and will herself there.

But as she considered the possibilities, a voice spoke from the darkness around her.

Not yet, daughter. You are not ready for such journeys.

The voice was female, ancient, and utterly alien. It spoke with the authority of someone who had existed since the dawn of creation, who had watched stars be born and die and counted the passage of eons like heartbeats.

Mother? Alexis thought the word rather than speaking it, unsure if normal vocal communication was even possible in this place.

I am here. I am always here, watching over you as I have since before you were born. But you must not attempt such distance yet. Your control is too new, too untested. You could lose yourself in the space between spaces and never find your way back to the world of flesh.

I need answers. About what I am, about what's happening to me.

And you shall have them when the time is right. But patience, my child. The universe is vast and old and full of dangers you cannot yet comprehend. Do not risk yourself for knowledge that will come to you in its proper season.

When will that be?

The presence that might have been Nyx seemed to smile, though Alexis had no way of seeing it in the perfect darkness of the ether.

Sooner than you think. But for now, return to your world. Return to the boy who watches over you with such devotion. He is more important than you know.

Before Alexis could ask what that meant, the ether released her, depositing her back in her yard with enough force to send her staggering. Keats was on his feet instantly, reaching out to steady her.

"Al? What happened? You were gone for like thirty seconds and then you just appeared out of nowhere looking like you'd seen a ghost."

"Not a ghost." She accepted his support gratefully; her legs still unsteady from the transition. "My mother. I think. Maybe. It's complicated."

"The goddess mother or the human mother?"

"Goddess. Definitely goddess." She sank onto the porch steps, trying to process what had just happened. "She spoke to me in the ether. Warned me not to try traveling long distances yet because I could get lost."

"Well, that's terrifying and reassuring at the same time." Keats settled beside her, close enough that she could feel the warmth radiating from his body. "Terrifying because apparently you can get lost in interdimensional space, reassuring because you've got a cosmic mother looking out for you."

"She said you were important. More important than I know." Alexis studied his profile in the starlight. "Any idea what that might mean?"

"Probably just that I'm your anchor to the normal world. The thing that keeps you grounded when cosmic weirdness threatens to sweep you away." He shrugged, but she caught the pleased flush that crept up his neck. "Or maybe I'm secretly part divine too and just haven't figured it out yet."

The joke was meant to lighten the mood, but it raised a question that had been nagging at her since their conversation with Hough. If Scions were drawn to each other, if power recognized power, then what did it say about Keats that he had been her closest friend for twelve years? What did it say about his uncanny reflexes, his ability to read her emotions, his absolute acceptance of supernatural impossibilities?

Before she could voice the question, the porch light flicked on, and Charles appeared in the doorway. He looked older than his fifty-three years, worn down by grief and secrets and the weight of protecting a daughter who was becoming something beyond his understanding.

"I thought I heard voices," he said, stepping onto the porch in pajamas and slippers. "Everything okay?"

"Just talking," Alexis replied, which was technically true even if it omitted the part about stepping into alternate dimensions.

Charles nodded, but his expression suggested he knew there was more to the story. "It's late. You two should probably head inside."

"Actually, I should get home," Keats said, standing and brushing grass from his jeans. "Mom's working a double shift, but she'll want to hear all the details when she gets back."

He headed for his car but paused at the edge of the driveway. "Al? Be careful with the stepping thing, okay? I meant what I said about not knowing your limits."

"I will."

"And don't make any major decisions without talking to me first. Promise?"

"Promise."

He drove away, leaving Alexis alone with her father and the weight of everything she could not tell him. Charles waited until the taillights disappeared around the corner before speaking.

"He's a good friend," he said quietly. "The kind of person who'll stand by you no matter what happens. Don't take that for granted."

"I won't."

"Good." He turned to go inside, then paused. "Your mother—Elizabeth—she always said you were destined for great things. I used to think she meant college, career, the normal kind of success. Now I'm starting to wonder if she knew more than she let on."

The words hung in the air between them, heavy with implication. Alexis wanted to ask what he meant, wanted to push for details about the conversations he and Elizabeth might have had about her future. But she could see the exhaustion in his face, the way grief had carved new lines around his eyes.

"Get some sleep, Dad," she said instead. "We'll figure everything out in the morning."

He nodded and disappeared into the house, leaving her alone under the stars. Above her, the night sky stretched infinite and welcoming, filled with possibilities she was only beginning to understand.

Somewhere in that darkness, ancient powers were watching. Waiting. Planning moves in a game whose rules she did not yet know and whose stakes she couldn't comprehend.

But for the first time since Elizabeth's death, she felt like she wasn't facing the unknown alone. She had Keats, steadfast and loyal and more important than she knew. She had Charles, struggling to protect her despite his human limitations. And she had a mother—a real mother—who spoke to her from the spaces between worlds.

It wasn't enough to guarantee safety, but it was enough to give her hope.

And in a world where the children of gods usually died screaming, hope was no small thing.

CHAPTER 7: DIVINE WRATH

Dr. Marcus Hough stood in his kitchen, pouring three fingers of bourbon into a crystal tumbler with hands that trembled despite his best efforts to keep them steady. The amber liquid sloshed against the glass, and he had to grip the bottle with both hands to keep from dropping it.

Alexis Rain had been gone for less than an hour, but her presence still lingered in his brownstone like the afterimage of lightning against closed eyelids. The girl—no, not a girl, something far more dangerous wearing the shape of one—had sat in his living room and asked questions with the casual confidence of someone who had never been denied answers.

The daughter of Nyx. A stable Scion. The first of her bloodline in recorded history.

He knocked back the bourbon in one burning gulp and immediately poured another.

The phone call had to be made. His contact would be expecting a report, and delays only led to suspicion. But the thought of describing what he'd seen, what he'd felt in her presence, made his stomach clench with something that might have been guilt or terror or both.

The girl had been so young. So normal-looking despite the power that radiated from her like heat from a forge. And her friend—the Keats boy—had watched her with the kind of devotion that spoke of genuine love rather than supernatural compulsion.

They had no idea what they were walking into.

Hough pulled out his phone and dialed the number he'd memorized but hoped never to use again. It rang twice before a voice answered—smooth, cultured, and absolutely cold.

"Dr. Hough. I trust your evening was... educational?"

"She was here. Just as you said she would be." Hough's voice came out steadier than he'd expected. "Alexis Rain. She's looking for information about her parentage."

"And you provided it?"

"I told her what you instructed me to tell her. About Scions, about the dangers they face. I gave her Rose Hartford's location in London."

"Excellent. How did she seem? Stable? Controlled?"

Hough thought about the way the air had shimmered around her when she'd grown frustrated, the subtle wrongness that had made his primitive hindbrain scream warnings about apex predators. "Very controlled. But there's something underneath, something powerful trying to get out. If she ever lost control completely..."

"Yes, that would be... problematic. But manageable, with the right preparation." The voice carried a note of satisfaction that made Hough's skin crawl. "You've done well, Doctor. Our arrangement continues to prove mutually beneficial."

"About that arrangement—" Hough began, but the line went dead before he could finish the thought.

He stared at the phone for a long moment, then set it on the counter and reached for the bourbon bottle again. The rational part of his mind—the part that had earned him tenure at Columbia—knew he was in too deep to back out now. But the human part, the part that remembered being a child afraid of monsters in the dark, wondered what he'd become in service to something that treated teenage girls as problems to be managed.

The bottle was halfway to his lips when the temperature in the kitchen dropped twenty degrees in the span of a heartbeat.

Frost began forming on the windows despite the late spring warmth outside. The overhead light flickered once, twice, then died completely, leaving him standing in darkness so absolute it seemed to have weight and texture.

"So. What are we going to do about this, Marcus?"

The voice came from everywhere and nowhere, resonating through his bones like the memory of sound rather than sound itself. Each word was a tiny knife sliding into his brain, precise and surgical and utterly without mercy.

Hough's breath came out in visible puffs as he turned toward the sound, though movement seemed pointless in darkness this complete. "Who—who's there?"

"You know who I am." The voice carried the authority of eons, of power that had existed since before humans learned to make fire. "The question is whether you know what you've done."

Understanding hit him like ice water in his veins. "Nyx."

"Very good, Doctor. I see your education wasn't entirely wasted." Something moved in the darkness—not seen but felt, a presence vast and terrible and utterly alien pressing against the boundaries of his sanity. "Tell me, do you truly believe you can hunt my daughter without consequences?"

"I'm not—I didn't—" He struggled for words, his academic training warring with primal terror. "I'm trying to help. To understand what she is, what she might become."

"Liar."

The word hit him like a physical blow, driving him to his knees on the kitchen floor. The bourbon glass shattered against the tiles, amber liquid spreading like blood in the starlight that filtered through frost-covered windows.

"You feed information to those who would destroy her. You play their games because you believe mortal concerns outweigh divine will." The presence moved closer, and Hough felt something that might have been breath against his neck—if beings like Nyx still needed to breathe. "So many poorly thought-out decisions, Marcus. That's what you've made."

"She's dangerous," he whispered, hating himself for the words even as they spilled out. "They all are. Scions, half-bloods, whatever you want to call them. They're aberrations, cosmic mistakes that threaten the natural order."

"Aberrations?" The temperature dropped another ten degrees, and ice began forming on the walls. "My child is no aberration. She is precisely what she was meant to be—a bridge between worlds, a force for change in a universe grown stagnant with mortal fears."

"But the others, the ones who went insane, who killed—"

"Were murdered." The words carried the finality of a closing tomb. "By people like you, Marcus. People who see power they cannot control and choose destruction over understanding. Simply out of nothing more than fear. People who mistake their own limitations for universal law."

Hough tried to stand, but his legs refused to obey. The darkness pressed down on him like the weight of the ocean, and he realized with crystalline clarity that he was about to die. Not quickly, not painlessly, but slowly and deliberately, as a lesson to others who might make similar choices.

"Please," he gasped. "I was trying to protect—"

"Protect whom? Certainly not the children you helped them locate. Certainly not the families torn apart by your intelligence." The presence circled him now, predator evaluating prey. "How many, Marcus? How many young lives lost because you provided names and addresses to those who hunt my kind?"

The number sat in his memory like a cancer: twenty-three. Twenty-three Scions identified, located, eliminated over the past five years. Young people who had committed no crime beyond being born with divine blood in their veins.

He'd told himself it was necessary. That they were ticking time bombs who would eventually explode and take innocent people with them. That the greater good required their sacrifice.

Now, faced with the reality of divine justice, those justifications felt thin as tissue paper.

"I was wrong," he whispered. "I was scared, and I was wrong."

"Yes. You were." The voice grew softer, almost gentle, which somehow made it infinitely more terrifying. "But fear, while understandable, does not excuse the choices you made. Actions have consequences, Marcus. Even for tenured professors with good intentions."

The darkness began to coalesce, taking on weight and substance. Hough felt invisible hands grasping at his throat, his chest, his mind. Not to kill—not yet—but to examine. To catalog every secret he'd kept, every betrayal he'd enabled, every life he'd helped destroy.

"You will make no more calls," the voice commanded. "You will provide no more information. You will discover that your phone no longer functions, your computer no longer connects to the internet, your ability to communicate with those who employ you has been... severed."

"And if I try to warn them? To contact them through other means?"

"Then you will learn why even Zeus fears to anger me." The presence withdrew slightly, giving him room to breathe but not to flee. "I am Nyx, primordial goddess of night. I am darkness given form, shadow given will. I existed before your species was but a thought, and I will exist long after your sun burns cold. Do not test my patience further."

The temperature began to rise, though the frost on the windows remained. Light seeped back into the kitchen by degrees, revealing a room that looked exactly as it had before—except for the shattered bourbon glass and the man kneeling among its fragments.

"You have a choice now, Marcus." The voice was fading, becoming distant and ethereal. "You can spend your remaining years in quiet retirement, troubled only by nightmares of the children whose deaths you enabled. Or you can continue to serve those who hunt my daughter, and discover that there are worse things than nightmares."

"What about Alexis? What about the danger she represents?"

"My daughter will choose her own path, as all children must. But she will do so free from the interference of mortals who mistake fear for wisdom." The presence was almost gone now, leaving only the memory of vast, implacable power. "Do not make me regret showing you mercy, Doctor. I am not known for giving second chances."

Silence fell over the kitchen like a blanket, broken only by Hough's ragged breathing and the tick of the clock on the wall. He remained kneeling among the glass fragments for a long time, staring at his hands and trying to process what had just happened.

He had faced a primordial goddess and lived. That was something, he supposed. A small victory in what felt like total defeat.

But as he finally stood and began cleaning up the bourbon and glass, Marcus Hough realized that survival wasn't the same as redemption. Twenty-three children were still dead because of his choices. Twenty-three families still mourned children who might have lived if he'd chosen courage over fear.

The goddess had offered him mercy, but mercy wasn't the same as forgiveness.

That would have to come from somewhere else entirely.

Outside the brownstone, shadows lengthened and deepened despite the streetlights' steady glow. In those shadows, something vast and patient settled in to watch. Not to threaten—the message had been delivered—but to ensure that Dr. Marcus Hough remembered the weight of divine attention.

Nyx had other children to protect, other threats to evaluate. But for now, this small corner of the mortal world was secure.

Her daughter could continue her journey toward understanding without interference from misguided academics and their genocidal employers.

The real challenges would come soon enough.

CHAPTER 8: FINALITY OF LOSS

Alexis had come down from her perch. She needed a walk in the cool night air, to clear her head and organize her thoughts. The mile-long road from Keats's house to her own had always been Alexis's favorite path to walk. The tree-lined streets of Mount Pleasant transformed after dark, becoming something deeper and more mysterious than their daytime suburban normalcy. Tonight, with her father's revelations and warnings still churning in her mind and power humming beneath her skin like electricity, the familiar route felt like a pilgrimage.

She was still a bit flabbergasted at how well Keats and his mom had taken all of this. Both of them were definitely trying to process the impossible things they'd learned over the past few days. Katy had taken the supernatural revelations with the same calm efficiency she brought to medical emergencies, asking practical questions about Alexis's abilities and safety rather than dwelling on the impossibility of it all. But even her steady presence couldn't quiet the restless energy that had been building in Alexis since her confrontation with Dr. Hough.

The night air held the warmth of late spring, carrying the scent of honeysuckle and new grass on a breeze that seemed to curl around her like a welcoming embrace.

The few streetlights that lined the road created distinct pools of amber illumination every fifty yards, but Alexis found herself drawn to the spaces between—the patches of shadow where the darkness felt most alive.

"Why?" she asked aloud, her voice barely above a whisper but somehow carrying the weight of eighteen years of questions. "If you are my real mother, how could you have left me here alone for so long? How could you have ignored me, let me feel like such a freak?"

The wind shifted, lifting strands of her hair across her face in what might have been an answer or might have been coincidence. But as it did, she felt something vast and patient stirring in the darkness around her—not visible, not quite audible, but undeniably present.

I have never left you, daughter.

The voice came from everywhere and nowhere, carried on currents of air that tasted of starlight and infinite space. It was the same presence she'd encountered in the ether, ancient and alien and absolutely certain of its own authority.

"Then where were you when I needed you?" The words spilled out before she could stop them, carrying all the accumulated hurt of a childhood spent feeling displaced and different. "Where were you when I couldn't cry at my mother's funeral? When I didn't understand why I remembered everything but couldn't connect with anyone? When I sat on my roof night after night wondering why I felt more at home in darkness than daylight?"

Learning. Growing. Becoming what you were meant to be. The presence grew stronger, and shadows began to lengthen despite the steady glow of streetlights. *The divine and mortal cannot be safely merged through force, child. It must happen naturally, gradually, or the vessel breaks under the strain.*

"Like Rose Hartford?"

Like so many others. There was genuine sadness in the cosmic voice now, the weight of eons spent watching children break under power they weren't ready to contain. *You have survived what destroys most of our kind because you were raised with love, with stability, with the patient guidance of those who cared more for your welfare than their own fear.*

Alexis thought of Charles and Elizabeth, of the careful normalcy they'd maintained even as impossible things happened around their adopted daughter. Of Keats, who had accepted her strangeness without question and stood by her even when that strangeness turned dangerous.

"They're not my real family," she said, though the words felt like betrayal even as she spoke them.

Are they not? The question carried gentle rebuke. *Biology creates potential, child. Love creates family. Charles Rain has been your father in every way that matters, just as Elizabeth was your mother. That she was not present at your conception does not diminish the truth of what she gave you.*

The wind died suddenly, leaving the street eerily quiet except for the distant hum of air conditioners and the soft rustle of leaves. Alexis felt the presence beginning to withdraw, slipping back into whatever cosmic realm it normally inhabited.

"Wait," she called out, panic flaring in her chest. "Don't go. I have so many questions—"

And you will have answers, when the time is right. But that time is not yet. The voice was growing fainter, more distant. *Be patient, daughter. Trust in the love that has sustained you thus far. And remember—darkness is not the absence of light. It is the canvas upon which light creates meaning.*

"What does that mean?"

But there was no answer. The presence was gone, leaving Alexis standing alone under the streetlights with nothing but the echo of cosmic wisdom she didn't understand and a heart full of questions that would have to wait for answers.

She resumed walking, but the familiar streets no longer felt welcoming. Instead, they felt small and confining, like a stage set that had been adequate for the opening acts but was now too limited for the main performance. Every house represented a life bound by mortal concerns—mortgage payments and school schedules and weekend barbecues—while she carried the blood of beings who had shaped the cosmos itself.

The isolation was crushing.

By the time she reached her own street, the restless energy had transformed into something darker and more desperate. She needed to talk to Charles, to make him understand that half-truths and careful omissions weren't enough anymore. She needed real answers about her heritage, about the forces that were moving against Scions, about what she was supposed to do with power that felt like carrying lightning in her bare hands.

The front door stood open.

Alexis stopped at the edge of the driveway, every instinct suddenly screaming warnings. Charles Rain didn't leave doors open. He checked locks twice before going to bed, made sure windows were latched, kept a baseball bat by his nightstand despite living in one of the safest neighborhoods in North Carolina.

She approached the house like she was walking through a minefield, every step careful and deliberate. The porch light was off, though she was certain it had been on when she left. Through the open doorway, she could see into the living room where a single lamp cast harsh shadows across overturned furniture.

"Dad?" she called, but got no answer.

The smell hit her as soon as she crossed the threshold—copper and something else, something organic and wrong that made her stomach clench with recognition even though she'd never encountered it before. The living room looked like a tornado had passed through it. Coffee table overturned, couch cushions scattered, books and magazines strewn across the floor in chaotic patterns that spoke of violent struggle.

She found him in the hallway between the living room and kitchen.

Her father lay motionless, twisted at an impossible angle. His neck bent wrong and his eyes stared blindly at the ceiling. Blood pooled beneath his head, dark and still congealing, suggesting he'd been dead for almost an hour. Which means it must have happened just after she left. His hands were scraped and bruised, evidence that he'd fought ferociously against his attacker before losing.

The sight should have sent her into shock, should have triggered the same emotional numbness that had protected her after Elizabeth's death. Instead, it ignited something primal and terrible in her chest.

Rage.

Pure, cosmic fury that burned away rational thought and left only the need to destroy whatever had done this. The ethereal luminescence that had occurred before from her very skin exploded from her like a miniature sun, silver light pouring from her skin in waves that made the air itself scream. The house and surrounding area lit up as if at the center of a ocean-side lighthouse.

When the initial surge passed, she found herself standing with her father's body at her feet. The smell of ozone hung heavy in the air.

"I'm sorry," she whispered, dropping to her knees beside Charles. "I'm so sorry I wasn't here."

But even as grief threatened to overwhelm her, another part of her mind was analyzing the scene with cold precision. The violence of the struggle, the way furniture had been overturned, the defensive wounds on Charles's hands—this hadn't been a random break-in or a robbery gone wrong. Someone had come here looking for something, and when Charles had tried to stop them, they'd killed him without hesitation.

Someone who knew about Alexis, about what she was becoming.

Someone like Pitts.

She pulled out her phone with hands that trembled only slightly and dialed 911. The conversation was brief and mechanical—address, nature of emergency, confirmation that she was safe and would wait for responders. Training from eighteen years of being Charles Rain's daughter kicked in, guiding her through the necessary steps while her heart shattered into pieces too small to reassemble.

The police arrived first, followed by paramedics who confirmed what she already knew. Detective Morrison, a tired-looking man in his fifties who had probably seen too many crime scenes in his career, asked gentle questions about Charles's enemies, his business dealings, anything that might explain why someone would want him dead.

Alexis answered honestly while carefully omitting any mention of supernatural stalkers or divine heritage. Yes, her father had seemed worried lately. No, she didn't know of any specific threats. Yes, she would be staying with friends until other arrangements could be made.

The lies came easily, protecting secrets that could never be shared with well-meaning mortals who had no frame of reference for cosmic conflicts.

By the time the coroner's van pulled away with Charles's body, Alexis had already made her decision. Grief would come later, when she had time to process the magnitude of her loss. Right now, there was only cold fury and the absolute certainty that whoever had done this would pay for it.

Keats arrived as the last police car was leaving, his face pale with shock as he took in the broken windows and official vehicles. He didn't ask questions, didn't demand explanations. He simply wrapped her in a fierce hug and held on while she stood rigid in his arms, afraid that if she let herself feel anything she might lose control again.

"We'll find them," he said quietly, his voice carrying deadly certainty. "Whoever did this, we'll find them and make them pay."

"I know." She pulled back to meet his eyes, seeing her own rage reflected there. "But first, we need to get stronger. We need to learn what I'm really capable of."

"What are you thinking?"

"I'm thinking it's time to stop playing defense." Power stirred beneath her skin like a caged predator, responding to her emotional state. "Someone wants a war with the daughter of Nyx? Fine. Let's give them one."

As they walked away from the house that had been her home for eighteen years, Alexis felt the last of her childhood burning away like paper in flame. She was no longer the confused teenager who couldn't cry at her mother's funeral or the frightened girl who had been stalked by supernatural forces beyond her understanding.

She was something else now. Something harder and more dangerous.

Something that understood the true meaning of loss, and was prepared to make others understand it, too.

Behind them, shadows lengthened across the crime scene despite the harsh glare of police lights. In those shadows, something vast and patient watched the last innocent daughter of Nyx disappear into the night.

The game had changed.

And the players were about to learn that some losses could never be forgiven.

CHAPTER 9: DONE HIDING

The funeral director had done his best to disguise the violence of Charles Rain's death, but Alexis could still see the subtle signs—the careful arrangement of his collar to hide off-color from bruising, the waxy texture of makeup applied too heavily around his temple and the sites of bruising. She stood beside the mahogany casket in the same church where they'd buried Elizabeth just two weeks ago, watching mourners file past to pay their respects, and felt nothing but cold fury wrapped in a thin veneer of civilized grief.

Detective Morrison stood near the back of the crowd, his presence a reminder that Charles's murder remained unsolved and likely always would. How could mortal law enforcement investigate a crime committed by beings who could step between dimensions and vanish at will? How could they track killers who left no forensic evidence because they barely existed in the physical world to begin with?

They couldn't. Which meant justice would have to come from other sources.

"He was a good man," Mrs. Patterson said, approaching with the careful steps of someone who had attended too many funerals in recent years. "Salt of the earth, as my grandmother used to say. The kind of person who made the world a little bit better just by being in it."

Alexis nodded and made appropriate sounds, but her attention was divided between maintaining polite conversation and keeping her abilities locked down. Grief mixed with rage was a volatile combination, and twice already she'd felt power surge toward the surface in response to well-meaning condolences that felt like salt in an open wound.

The air around her shimmered with barely contained energy, and she noticed how people unconsciously stepped back when they got too close, some primitive part of their brains recognizing the presence of something dangerous. Only Keats seemed immune to the effect, standing at her left shoulder like an anchor point in a world that felt increasingly unstable.

"You holding up okay?" he asked quietly during a lull in the receiving line.

"Define okay." Her voice came out flat, emotionless. "If you mean am I successfully resisting the urge to incinerate everyone who tells me my father is 'in a better place now,' then yes. Barely."

"That's something, I guess." He studied her profile with the kind of attention he'd been giving her since childhood, cataloguing micro-expressions that most people would miss. "You look like you're about to either explode or implode."

"Both, probably." She watched the funeral director signal that it was time to move to the graveside service. "I keep thinking he should be here. Dad, I mean. He should be the one organizing this, making sure everything runs smoothly, taking care of everyone else like he always did."

"Instead, you're doing it."

"Because there's no one else left." The words carried a finality that went beyond logistics. Charles's death hadn't just orphaned her—it had severed her last connection to the normal world, cut the final anchor that had kept her tethered to human concerns and limitations.

The graveside service was mercifully brief. Pastor Williams spoke about eternal rest and divine plans, words that rang hollow to someone who had recently learned that divine plans involved considerably more violence and manipulation than most people imagined. Alexis stood through the prayers and hymns with mechanical precision, her mind already moving beyond grief toward more practical concerns.

When the last mourner had departed and the cemetery workers began their final preparations, she remained by the grave with Keats and Katy, staring at the polished headstone that read "Charles Michael Rain: Beloved Husband and Father."

"What now?" Katy asked gently. "You know you're welcome to stay with us as long as you need."

"I know. And I'm grateful." Alexis turned away from the grave, decision crystallizing in her mind with the clarity that came from having no good options left. "But I can't stay. Not if I want to keep you both safe."

"Al—" Keats started.

"No." She cut him off before he could voice the objection she saw forming. "Think about what happened to Dad. Think about what Pitts is capable of. As long as I'm around normal people, I'm putting them at risk. And I won't lose anyone else because they were unlucky enough to care about me."

"So what's the alternative?" Katy's nurse training showed in the way she approached problems—practical, methodical, focused on solutions rather than emotions. "You can't just disappear into the supernatural underground. You're eighteen years old."

"I'm eighteen years old with access to a trust fund worth more than most people see in a lifetime." Alexis started walking toward the parking lot, her mind already working through logistics. "Money solves a lot of problems, including the problem of how to operate independently while tracking down cosmic-level threats."

The drive back to Mount Pleasant passed in tense silence, each of them lost in their own thoughts about what came next. Alexis stared out the window at familiar streets and landmarks, cataloguing details she might never see again. The town that had shaped her childhood suddenly felt small and fragile, like a paper model that could be destroyed by careless handling.

By the time they reached the Keats' house, she had made her decision.

"I need to make some phone calls," she announced, pulling out her phone. "And I'll need to borrow your computer."

"For what?" Keats asked, though his expression suggested he already knew he wouldn't like the answer.

"To liquidate everything. House, investments, insurance policies—all of it. I want every asset my parents left converted to cash or easily portable securities." She scrolled through her contacts, looking for the number of the family attorney. "If I'm going after whoever killed them, I'll need resources that can't be frozen or traced."

"Alexis." Katy's voice carried the kind of authority that came from years of dealing with patients in crisis. "You need to slow down and think about this rationally. You've just buried your father. You're traumatized, you're angry, and you're making decisions that could affect the rest of your life."

"My life changed the moment Mom died in that car accident. It changed again when Dad was murdered in our living room." Alexis met the older woman's gaze steadily. "I'm not making emotional decisions, Katy. I'm making strategic ones. The people who killed my parents aren't going to stop because I'm grieving. They're going to keep coming, and when they do, I want to be ready."

"Ready for what?"

"War."

The word hung in the air like a challenge, stark and uncompromising. Keats shifted uncomfortably, while Katy's expression grew troubled in the way that suggested she was seeing unwelcome parallels to other young people who had chosen violence over healing.

"Violence isn't always the answer," she said carefully.

"Maybe not. But it's the only language some people understand." Alexis pulled up her attorney's number and pressed call. "And since diplomatic solutions don't seem to be working out so well for my family, I think it's time to try a more direct approach."

The conversation with Harold Mason, Esquire, was brief and to the point. Yes, she wanted to liquidate the entire estate. Yes, she understood the tax implications. No, she didn't want to discuss the wisdom of such a decision during a period of emotional distress.

By the time she hung up, the first phase of her plan was already in motion.

"The house should sell quickly," she told Keats, who had been listening with growing alarm. "It's in a good neighborhood, and real estate is moving fast right now. Mason estimates I'll have access to liquid assets within two weeks, three at the outside."

"And then what? You just vanish into the night like some kind of supernatural vigilante?"

"Then I start getting answers. About what I am, about who's hunting Scions, about how to fight back effectively." She pulled up airline websites on her phone, checking availability for international flights. "Dr. Hough mentioned Rose Hartford in London. That seems like a good place to start."

"I'm coming with you."

The declaration was quiet but absolute, carrying the kind of certainty that brooked no argument. Alexis looked up from her phone to find Keats watching her with an expression she'd never seen before—determined, protective, and slightly dangerous.

"Keats—"

"Don't." He held up a hand to forestall her objection. "We've been best friends for twelve years. We've been through everything together—school, family drama, your weird supernatural awakening, multiple deaths. You really think I'm going to let you face whatever comes next alone?"

"It's not safe."

"Neither is staying here while cosmic forces hunt down everyone I care about." His jaw set with stubborn determination. "Besides, you said it yourself—you need resources. Well, I've got a trust fund too. Not as big as yours, but big enough to be useful."

Katy looked back and forth between them like a referee watching a tennis match, her expression cycling through various forms of dismay. "You're both insane," she said finally. "Completely, utterly insane." Suddenly, she smiled. She looked from Keats to Alexis and back to Keats. "Be her sounding board. Be the voice of reason, if need be. Protect each other. At this point, nothing will stop her."

"Probably not," Alexis agreed. "I suppose insanity seems to be a survival trait in my family."

The rest of the afternoon passed in a blur of phone calls and online forms as Alexis systematically dismantled the infrastructure of her normal life. Bank accounts consolidated. Investment portfolios liquidated. Insurance claims filed. College enrollment deferred indefinitely.

Each transaction felt like cutting another tie to the world she'd grown up in, but also like shedding weight that had been holding her back. A week later, the process was largely complete, leaving her feeling simultaneously liberated and terrified.

"Last chance to change your mind," she told Keats as they sat on his front porch, watching the sun set over the neighborhood that had been their whole world for most of their lives.

"Not happening." He leaned back in his chair, projecting a calm he probably didn't feel. "Though I have to ask—do you have any kind of plan beyond 'go to London and hope the crazy lady has answers'?"

"I have the beginning of a plan." She pulled out a notebook where she'd been sketching ideas throughout the day. "Phase one: learn everything I can about what I am and what I'm capable of. Phase two: identify the people responsible for my parents' deaths. Phase three: make them pay."

"That's not really a plan so much as a to-do list."

"It's a start." She closed the notebook and stood up, decision made. "The rest we'll figure out as we go."

As they headed inside to prepare for a journey that would take them far from everything familiar, Alexis felt the last vestiges of her old life falling away like shed skin. The girl who had worried about college applications and graduation ceremonies was gone, replaced by something harder and more purposeful.

She was no longer Alexis Rain, small-town teenager with a strange gift for memory.

She was the daughter of Nyx, and she was finally ready to claim that inheritance.

Even if it destroyed her in the process.

Later that night, as Keats slept in the guest room and Katy worked her shift at the hospital, Alexis stood in the backyard staring up at the star-filled sky. Tomorrow, they would prepare for London and step fully into the supernatural world that had been calling to her since birth.

"I hope you're watching," she whispered to the darkness. "Because I'm done hiding. I'm done pretending to be something I'm not. And I'm done letting other people pay the price for what I am."

The wind stirred around her, carrying scents of honeysuckle and distant rain. For a moment, she thought she felt that vast, patient presence that might have been her divine mother, offering wordless approval for the path she'd chosen.

But when the breeze died down, she was alone again with her plans and her rage and the absolute certainty that nothing would ever be the same.

Which was exactly what she wanted.

CHAPTER 10: BOUND BY DIVINE BLOOD

The woman appeared on Katy's front porch at exactly noon, materializing between one moment and the next like she'd stepped out of a fold in reality itself. Alexis felt the arrival like a physical pressure against her consciousness—divine power recognizing divine power across the barriers of mortal space.

"Someone's here," she announced, moving toward the window. "Someone like me."

Keats looked up from his laptop where he'd been researching St. Anne's Care Facility. "Like you how?"

"Divine. Powerful. And really, really bright."

As if summoned by her words, light blazed through the windows with the intensity of a solar flare, forcing both teenagers to shield their eyes. When the radiance faded to manageable levels, they found themselves staring at a woman who looked like she'd been carved from sunlight and given human form.

She was tall—easily six feet—with golden hair that moved in currents of air that touched nothing else, and skin that seemed to generate its own luminescence. Her clothes were simple—white linen dress, sandals that looked handmade—but they carried an aura of timeless elegance that made fashion seem irrelevant.

Most unsettling were her eyes, which held the warm yellow-gold of summer afternoons and seemed to see through flesh and bone to whatever lay beneath.

"May I come in?" she asked, her voice carrying the authority of someone accustomed to being obeyed without question. "We have much to discuss, sister."

Sister.

The word hit Alexis like a punch to the solar plexus. She'd known, intellectually, that having a divine mother likely meant having divine siblings. But knowing something in theory was vastly different from facing the reality of family members who could bend light to their will.

"Alexis?" Keats's voice carried a warning edge. "Should I be reaching for weapons right now?"

"I don't think weapons would help." She moved to unlock the front door, every instinct screaming caution while curiosity overrode common sense. "But stay close."

The woman—goddess—stepped across the threshold with the fluid grace of someone to whom physical laws were merely suggestions. Up close, her presence was even more overwhelming, like standing too near a bonfire that burned with divine rather than earthly flame.

"You may call me Mera," she said, settling onto Katy's couch with the casual confidence of visiting royalty. "Though mortals have known me by other names. Hemera. Aurora. The personification of day itself."

"Day," Alexis repeated, pieces of mythological knowledge clicking into place. "You're the goddess of day. Which makes you..."

"Your half-sister, yes. We share a mother, though you had an actual father." Alexis ran questions through her mind and learned that Nyx had apparently birthed many of her offspring without any need of a father. "I've come because your recent activities have attracted attention in certain circles."

"What kind of attention?"

"The kind that matters." Mera gestured, and the air around her shimmered with heat distortion despite the air conditioning. "Zeus himself has taken notice of Nyx's daughter. The Olympian Council has been... discussing your situation."

The implications of that statement made Alexis's mouth go dry. "Discussing it how?"

"Some view you as an unprecedented opportunity. The first stable Scion of primordial blood in recorded history, a bridge between the ancient powers and the younger gods." Mera's golden eyes fixed on Alexis with laser intensity. "Others see you as a potential threat to the cosmic order that has maintained stability for millennia."

"And which side are you on?"

"I am on the side of family." The answer was immediate and absolute. "But family loyalty has its limits when universal stability is at stake."

Keats, who had been listening with growing tension, finally spoke up. "Are you here to threaten her?"

Mera turned her attention to him for the first time, and Alexis saw him flinch slightly under the weight of divine scrutiny. "I am here to educate her. Knowledge is power, young man, and power wielded in ignorance tends to create catastrophic consequences."

"Again," Alexis said, "Is that a threat?"

"I am stating fact." Mera's own radiance increased in response, and suddenly the living room felt like the inside of a furnace. "Divine blood carries both gifts and curses, sister. The sooner you accept that reality, the longer you're likely to survive it."

The standoff stretched for several seconds, divine power pressing against divine power while the mortal furniture began to smoke from the ambient heat. Finally, Alexis forced herself to step back, literally and figuratively.

"What do you want from me?"

"Understanding. Compliance with certain... protocols that govern supernatural affairs." Mera's radiance dimmed to more manageable levels. "There are laws, sister. Ancient compacts that prevent the divine realm from interfering directly in mortal affairs. Your father—Charles Rain—was protected by those laws. His murder represents a violation that cannot go unanswered."

"Then why hasn't it been answered?" The words came out harder than Alexis intended. "If these laws are so important, why is his killer still walking free?"

"Because the killer in question is also bound by divine blood, which complicates matters of justice considerably." Mera's expression grew troubled. "Phthonos—or Pitts, as he has taken to calling himself—is our half-brother. Son of Nyx and Erebus, god of envy and resentment. His actions have forced the Council to address questions they have been avoiding for centuries."

Half-brother. Another family member Alexis had never known existed, this one apparently a murderer with a grudge against the cosmic order. The supernatural soap opera of her parentage was becoming more complicated by the hour.

"What questions?"

"Whether Scions represent evolution or aberration. Whether the barriers between divine and mortal should be maintained or allowed to dissolve. Whether beings like you should be protected, eliminated, or controlled." Mera leaned forward, her intensity burning through the air like focused sunlight. "Your choices in the coming days will influence those debates significantly."

"No pressure or anything," Keats muttered.

"Indeed." Mera's attention shifted back to him. "Which brings me to my second purpose here. You cannot accompany her on this journey."

"Like hell I can't."

"Your presence will endanger not only yourself but her as well. The moment you set foot in London, every divine faction on the continent will know exactly where to find you both."

Alexis felt something cold settle in her stomach. "Is that true?"

"Regrettably, yes. The threat there is... considerable. Unshielded, your presence broadcasts across dimensional barriers like a lighthouse in fog." Mera stood, her business apparently concluded. "If you insist on this course of action, Keats must remain behind. Otherwise, his presence will allow for... variations in the timeline."

"Uh, what?"

"We've received word from other oracles. Yes, there are others. They've seen multiple visions, mostly the same, showing dramatic variation in the likelihood of your success, and survival, should he accompany you. Nyx's protection can prevent that."

"Her protection?"

"Did you think Nyx's influence was limited to cosmic distances? This entire town exists within her sphere of awareness. While you remain here, you are both relatively safe. The moment you leave..." She shrugged eloquently.

The casual revelation that her entire hometown was under divine surveillance should have been shocking. Instead, it felt like another piece of a puzzle falling into place. The way shadows had always felt welcoming, the sense of being watched that she'd attributed to paranoia, the feeling that Mount Pleasant existed slightly apart from the normal world.

"So, what are my options?" Alexis asked. "Stay here and learn nothing, or leave Keats behind and face whatever's waiting alone?"

"There is a third option." Mera stood and moved toward the door, her purpose apparently served. "Develop your abilities to their full potential before attempting to engage with other supernatural forces. A daughter of Nyx who can access her true power has little to fear from younger gods or their servants."

"And how exactly do I do that?"

"Practice. Experimentation. Careful exploration of your inherited abilities." Mera paused at the threshold. "The ether responds to will and intention, sister. But, you must master those things. Master them, and distance becomes irrelevant."

She stepped outside and vanished in a burst of golden light that left spots dancing across Alexis's vision. When her sight cleared, she found Keats staring at her with an expression that mixed determination with barely controlled fear.

"So," he said finally. "Want to tell me more about this ether thing?"

They spent the afternoon in Katy's backyard, systematically testing the limits of Alexis's transportation abilities while trying to process everything Mera had revealed. The practice sessions were frustrating—Alexis could consistently access the ether now, but actually navigating it remained hit-or-miss.

"Try thinking about a specific location," Keats suggested as she materialized from her fifth attempt to reach the other side of town. "Not just 'somewhere else,' but an exact place with details you can visualize."

"I am visualizing." She wiped sweat from her forehead, the dimensional transitions taking more out of her than she'd expected. "The problem is that distance doesn't work the same way in there. Everything feels equally far and equally close."

"Maybe that's the point. Maybe distance is a physical limitation that doesn't apply to whatever dimension you're accessing."

The suggestion sparked something in her memory—fragments of knowledge that might have come from her own research or might have been inherited along with her divine blood. The ether wasn't bound by conventional space-time. Movement through it was governed by will and intention rather than physics.

"Let me try something different," she said, closing her eyes and focusing not on a destination but on a purpose. Not where she wanted to go, but why she wanted to go there.

The transition was smoother this time, like stepping through a doorway rather than forcing her way through resistant matter. The ether welcomed her with its familiar grayness, but now she could sense the pathways that connected it to the physical world—threads of possibility that led to every location she could clearly envision.

She chose one at random and stepped through.

"Jesus Christ!" Keats's voice came from behind her, and she turned to find him standing in what was definitely not Katy's backyard. Instead, they were on the observation deck of the Empire State Building, with the sprawling vista of Manhattan stretching out below them.

"How did you—" she started, then stopped as she realized the implications. "You came through with me."

"I was touching your arm when you vanished. Apparently, that was enough." He looked around in wonder mixed with terror. "Al, we're in New York. We just traveled six hundred miles in the space of a heartbeat."

"Mera said we were beacons to supernatural predators when we travel." Alexis felt power building around them both, responding to the emotional intensity of the moment. "If she's right, then every divine faction on the East Coast just felt us arrive."

As if summoned by her words, the air around them began to shimmer with displaced energy. Not the familiar silver-black of her own power, but something else—multiple something elses, approaching fast from various directions.

"Time to go," Keats said, grabbing her hand.

"Where?"

"Anywhere but here."

Alexis reached for the ether again, but this time the transition felt different—harder, like pushing through molasses instead of stepping through water. Something was interfering with her abilities, dampening her connection to the dimensional pathways.

Around them, the shimmering intensified, and she caught glimpses of figures materializing on the observation deck—tall, luminous beings that radiated power and authority in waves that made her knees weak.

"Now would be good," Keats said urgently.

She pushed harder, forcing her way into the ether through whatever interference was blocking her path. The darkness embraced them both, and she focused every ounce of will on a single destination: home.

They materialized in Katy's backyard hard enough to leave crater-shaped impressions in the lawn. Alexis rolled away from the impact, her entire body aching from the forced transition, while Keats lay gasping beside her.

"That," he said when he could speak again, "was both the most amazing and most terrifying thing I've ever experienced."

"It's getting easier." Alexis sat up, testing her connection to the ether. The familiar pathways were clear again, no longer blocked by whatever interference they'd encountered in New York. "But Mera was right about one thing—traveling with you is like sending up a flare to every supernatural being within a thousand miles."

"So, we need to figure out how to shield me." He stood up, brushing dirt from his clothes. "Because I'm not letting you face this alone, beacon or no beacon."

"Keats—"

"Non-negotiable." His expression carried the same stubborn determination she'd seen at the funeral. "We're in this together, remember?"

Alexis wanted to argue, wanted to find some way to keep him safe while she ventured into increasingly dangerous territory. But the truth was, she needed him. Not just for emotional support, but for the perspective he brought to impossible situations and the way he could see possibilities she missed.

"Okay," she said finally. "But we do this smart. No more blind jumps to random locations. We plan, we prepare, and we make sure we understand what we're walking into before we take any more interdimensional field trips."

"Agreed. So what's our first step?"

Alexis looked up at the sky, where the sun was beginning to set despite the early hour. Evening was coming, and with it the darkness that called to her like home. Soon, she would be at full strength, connected to powers that had existed since the dawn of creation.

"We learn everything we can about my celestial family," she said. "The good ones and the bad ones. Because something tells me we're going to be meeting them all soon enough."

As if in response to her words, shadows began to lengthen across the yard despite the persistence of daylight. In those shadows, ancient powers stirred, taking notice of the daughter of Nyx who was finally learning to claim her inheritance.

The game was accelerating, and the stakes were rising with every manifestation of her abilities.

But for the first time since Elizabeth's death, Alexis felt like she had the smallest chance of winning.

CHAPTER 11: AMBUSH

St. Anne's Care Facility squatted against the London skyline like a Gothic monument to institutional despair. The Victorian brick facade, darkened by decades of industrial pollution, gave the building the appearance of a fortress designed to keep its inhabitants locked away from a world that couldn't understand their particular form of madness.

Alexis stood across the street from the main entrance, studying the facility's security measures while rain drummed steadily against her jacket hood. Three days of reconnaissance had revealed patterns in the staff rotations, blind spots in the camera coverage, and the fact that Rose Hartford was housed in the high-security wing reserved for patients deemed dangerous to themselves and others.

"Shift change in ten minutes," Keats said, checking his watch. "Guards will be distracted for about three minutes while they brief the incoming team."

"Enough time to get inside, assuming I can access the ether with you in tow." Alexis had been practicing dimensional travel with her friend for the past week, using London's extensive park system as a testing ground. The results were promising but inconsistent—sometimes Keats translated smoothly, other times he arrived disoriented and nauseous.

"And if you can't?"

"Then we abort and try again tomorrow." She pulled her hood up against the intensifying rain. "I'm not risking exposure for the sake of impatience."

They waited in the shadow of a construction scaffold, watching uniformed guards move through their evening routines with the mechanical precision of institutional employment. At exactly 8:17 PM, the day shift began filing out while the night crew gathered in the security office for their briefing.

"Now," Alexis said, reaching for Keats's hand.

The transition into the ether felt different with him along—heavier, more resistant, like dragging an anchor through cosmic darkness. But the pathways were clear, and she focused on the destination she'd been visualizing all week: Rose Hartford's room on the facility's third floor.

They materialized in a space that looked more like a prison cell than a medical facility. Concrete walls painted institutional green, a narrow bed bolted to the floor, and a single window covered with mesh screening that turned the outside world into a collection of gray fragments.

Rose Hartford sat in the room's only chair, staring at a wall covered with intricate mathematical equations written in what appeared to be her own blood but was actually just red crayon. She was younger than Alexis had expected—maybe twenty-two—with prematurely gray-streaked auburn hair and the kind of hollow-eyed intensity that suggested too many thoughts moving too quickly through a mind that couldn't process them all.

"Visitors," Rose said without turning around. "How refreshing. Though I should warn you, the guards will be making rounds in seventeen minutes and thirty-four seconds. Unless you're here to kill me, in which case you should probably get started."

"We're not here to kill you." Alexis approached carefully, noting the way Rose's hands moved in constant, minute calculations—fingers tracing invisible equations in the air. "Dr. Hough sent us. We need information about Scions."

"Hough." Rose's laugh held no humor. "Dear Marcus, still playing puppet to forces he doesn't understand. Did he tell you what happens to most of us? The children of gods who inherit madness along with power?"

"He mentioned that the survival rate was low."

"Low." Rose finally turned to face them, and Alexis saw eyes that held the fractured brilliance of a mind operating on too many levels simultaneously. "Ninety-three point seven percent mortality rate before age twenty. Of the survivors, eighty-six percent develop severe psychological disorders within five years of manifestation. I am the daughter of Athena, goddess of wisdom and strategy. Do you know what divine wisdom looks like when filtered through a human brain?"

She gestured toward the equations covering the wall—complex mathematical proofs that seemed to shift and writhe when Alexis wasn't looking directly at them.

"I can see the underlying structure of reality," Rose continued. "The mathematical foundations that govern everything from quantum mechanics to divine politics. I know how many atoms are in this room, how many possible futures branch from this moment, exactly how long each of us will live if current probability matrices hold steady."

"That doesn't sound like madness," Keats said carefully. "That sounds like—"

"Like having access to information no mortal mind was designed to process." Rose's smile was sharp and broken. "The human brain can't handle that kind of data flow. It's like trying to download the entire internet through a coffee straw. Eventually, something breaks. Usually the straw."

She stood and moved to the window, her movements precise but somehow disconnected, as if she were piloting her body from a great distance. "But you didn't come here for a psychology lesson. You want to know about the conspiracy, about the systematic elimination of our kind."

"You know about that?"

"I know about everything. Past, present, probable futures." Rose pressed her palm against the mesh-covered glass. "They call themselves the Restoration Protocol. Mortals who believe divine blood should never have mixed with human genetics. They hunt us not from malice but from genuine belief that they're saving the world from contamination."

"Who leads them?"

"No one. Everyone. It's a hydra organization, cells operating independently but toward the same goal." Rose's reflection in the window seemed to flicker between sanity and madness. "But there's someone pulling strings from the shadows. Someone with enough divine blood to coordinate supernatural assets while remaining hidden from divine detection."

"Do you have a name?"

"Names have power. Power draws attention. Attention leads to consequences I've seen but would prefer to avoid." Rose turned back to them, her expression cycling through emotions too quickly to follow. "But I can give you something better than a name. I can give you a direction."

"What kind of direction?"

"The Caucasus Mountains. There's a facility there, hidden in the old Soviet ruins. They've been gathering artifacts, weapons designed to kill our kind. If you want to understand what you're fighting, that's where you need to go."

Keats frowned. "That seems awfully convenient. How do we know this isn't a trap?"

"You don't." Rose's smile turned genuinely amused. "But then, everything is a trap when you're hunting predators who've had centuries to prepare their snares. The question isn't whether you'll walk into traps—it's whether you'll be strong enough to break free when you do."

A distant alarm began sounding somewhere in the facility's depths. Rose tilted her head, listening to sounds only she could hear.

"Guards are coming early tonight. Someone's been watching the security feeds more carefully than usual." She moved back to her chair with the same disconnected precision. "You should leave. The information I've given you is accurate, but the people who want you dead are already moving to capitalize on your presence here."

"Come with us," Alexis said impulsively. "You don't have to stay in this place."

"Yes, I do." Rose settled into her chair and resumed staring at her blood-written equations. "This is the only place where the voices in my head are quiet enough for me to think. Out there, in the world, the data flow is too intense. I become... problematic."

"Rose—"

"Go." The command carried divine authority despite being spoken by someone locked in a psychiatric facility. "And remember—when you find what you're looking for in the Caucasus, don't trust anyone who claims to be offering help. In this war, everyone has their own agenda. Trust only one: Aaron Richardson. And, Alexis... Tell soldier boy that I miss him."

Footsteps echoed in the corridor outside, accompanied by the jangle of keys and radio chatter. Alexis grabbed Keats's hand and reached for the ether, pulling them both into dimensional transit just as the door burst open.

They materialized in an alley three blocks from the facility, both of them breathing hard from the adrenaline spike of narrow escape. Rain continued falling, washing away the institutional smell that had clung to their clothes.

"Well," Keats said finally. "That was illuminating and terrifying in equal measure."

"She's what I could become." Alexis leaned against the alley wall, processing the encounter. "If I can't learn to control the information flow, if the divine knowledge becomes too much for my human brain to handle."

"That's not going to happen."

"How can you be sure?"

"Because you're stronger than she is. You've had eighteen years to develop coping mechanisms for processing impossible amounts of information. Your perfect memory trained you to organize and compartmentalize data." Keats moved closer, his presence solid and reassuring in the rain-soaked darkness. "Besides, you're not alone in this. Rose is isolated, cut off from support systems. You have people who care about you."

The simple declaration carried more weight than any philosophical argument. Alexis had seen that Rose Hartford nearly destroyed herself with divine knowledge, seen what happened when cosmic inheritance overwhelmed human limitations. But she also had something Rose apparently lacked—connections to people who would anchor her to sanity when the universe tried to sweep her away.

"The Caucasus Mountains," she said, shifting focus back to actionable intelligence. "That's our next destination."

"Russia? Al, that's like jumping from the frying pan into the nuclear reactor. If there really is a facility there designed to kill Scions, walking in uninvited seems like a good way to get ourselves murdered."

"Probably. But Rose was right about one thing—we need to understand what we're fighting before we can figure out how to fight it effectively." She pulled out her phone and started researching the areas around the Caucasus. "Besides, my abilities are getting stronger every day. If there are weapons designed to kill people like me, I want to know about them before someone uses them against us."

"And if this is a trap? If someone's feeding Rose information designed to lure us into an ambush?"

"Then we'll deal with that when it happens. But, sitting here analyzing possibilities isn't going to get us answers. Sometimes you have to take calculated risks."

"This feels more like reckless endangerment than calculated risk."

"Welcome to my new life." She started reviewing the likely areas and then began running questions through her mind's catalog to narrow things down. "Trust me, Keats. I can feel that we're on the right track. Whatever's waiting for us in the Caucasus, it's connected to everything that's been happening. We just need to find this Aaron Richardson."

As they made their way back toward their hotel, neither of them noticed the figure watching from the shadows across the street. Or the way those shadows seemed to writhe and move independently of their light sources.

Some traps were set in motion long before the prey realized they were being hunted.

The next day, Alexis and Keats found themselves stepping into the country known as Dagestan, hiking through the remote reaches of the Caucasus, following the minute directions Rose had provided along with cryptic warnings about trusting their instincts over their technology. The landscape was breathtakingly beautiful—snow-capped peaks rising into crystal-clear air, forests that looked untouched by human presence, valleys carved by glaciers into patterns that seemed almost architectural in their precision.

It was also the perfect place for an ambush.

"I'm getting a bad feeling about this," Keats said as they crested a ridge that offered commanding views of the surrounding terrain. "Like, really bad. The kind of bad that makes me want to turn around and catch the next flight home."

"Your instincts kicking into high gear, huh?" Alexis asked, though she'd been fighting similar intuitions for the past hour.

"Maybe. Or maybe just common sense screaming that two teenagers with no military training shouldn't be wandering around former Soviet territory looking for secret weapons facilities." He checked their position on the GPS unit. "According to this, we're about two kilometers from the coordinates of the last known location of this Richardson guy. He sounds like a genteel individual."

"I suppose we'll see." Alexis scanned the valley below, noting terrain features that could provide cover or concealment. "But, you're right. Something feels wrong. Like we're being watched."

"Or herded." Keats's expression grew troubled. "What if this whole thing is designed to get us away from populated areas where we can't call for help?"

The possibility had occurred to her, but they'd already committed to the course of action. Turning back now would mean abandoning their best lead on the conspiracy that had killed her parents.

"We keep going," she decided. "But carefully. And at the first sign of trouble—"

The crack of a rifle shot echoed across the valley, and something whined through the air inches from her head. Alexis threw herself behind the nearest boulder as more shots followed, the impacts sending rock fragments spraying in all directions.

"Contact!" someone shouted in accented English. "Targets are in position. Beginning engagement."

Keats scrambled for cover beside her, his face pale with shock. "They were waiting for us. This whole thing was a setup!"

"Looks like it." Alexis risked a glance around the boulder and counted at least six muzzle flashes from different positions. Professional spacing, overlapping fields of fire, coordinated movement that spoke of military training. "They're trying to pin us down, probably so they can close for capture."

"What do we do?"

The question hung in the air between them, loaded with implications neither wanted to acknowledge. These weren't supernatural threats that could be reasoned with or divine powers that might show mercy. These were human soldiers with orders to kill or capture them, and they were clearly prepared for the possibility that their targets had unusual abilities.

"We fight," Alexis said finally, power beginning to build beneath her skin. "And we make sure we're the ones who walk away from this."

She stepped into the ether, using dimensional transit to appear behind the nearest sniper position. The man never saw her coming—one moment he was adjusting his scope, the next her hands were around his throat, divine strength crushing his windpipe before he could cry out.

The kill was quick, efficient, and absolutely necessary.

It was also the first time she had deliberately taken a human life.

The realization hit her like ice water as the sniper's body went limp in her arms. She was no longer an innocent teenager caught up in supernatural conflicts. She was a killer, someone who had crossed a line that could never be uncrossed.

But there was no time for psychological processing. Keats was still pinned down, and the remaining attackers were repositioning to deal with her flanking maneuver.

Alexis accessed the ether again, appearing behind a second position where two soldiers were coordinating their assault. These men were ready for her—they turned with inhuman speed, weapons tracking toward her position with precision that suggested enhanced reflexes or supernatural assistance.

She killed them both with bursts of silver fire that left nothing but ash and the smell of ozone. She didn't even know she could do that.

Keats had moved and was now engaged with one of the soldiers. All those years of martial arts training served him well and he managed a throat punch, a throw and a quick knee to the windpipe that ended the soldier's threat. He shook himself as if trying to remove water from his very soul and moved with his unusual quickness to meet the second soldier coming for him.

By the time the engagement ended, six bodies lay scattered across the mountainside, and Alexis knelt in the snow with blood on her hands and the taste of violence in her mouth. Keats appeared beside her, moving with the shell-shocked precision of someone processing trauma in real time.

"Are you hurt?" he asked, running his hands over her arms and shoulders, checking for wounds.

"No. You?"

"Physically? I'm fine." He looked around at the carnage, his expression cycling through emotions too complex to name. "Psychologically? I think I'm going to need some time to process what just happened."

Alexis understood the feeling. The necessity of the violence didn't erase the horror of it, didn't make the transition from defender to killer any easier to accept. They had both crossed a threshold today, entering a darker version of themselves that would be impossible to leave behind.

"We should search the bodies," she said, forcing herself to focus on practical concerns. "See if they have identification, communication equipment, anything that might tell us who sent them."

The search revealed military-grade weapons, tactical gear without national markings, and communication devices encrypted beyond their ability to decode. Professional soldiers, well-equipped and well-trained, who had been prepared for supernatural targets.

"Rose was right," Keats said, examining a specialized ammunition clip. "These rounds are designed for enhanced targets. Look at the bullet composition—silver core, blessed metals, inscription work that looks like protective wards."

"Someone's been doing their homework. Not that, I think, they would have worked on me...but a bullet is a bullet." Alexis pocketed the ammunition for later analysis. "The question is whether this was a trap from the beginning, or if we stumbled into a patrol that was already in the area."

"Does it matter? Either way, we're burned. They know we're here, they know what we're capable of, and they're probably calling for backup right now."

"Then we finish what we came for and get out." Alexis stood, decision crystallizing in her mind. "The facility Rose mentioned is still out there. If it really does contain weapons designed to kill Scions, I want to see them before we leave."

"Al, this is insane. We just killed six people. We're in hostile territory with limited resources and no backup. The smart thing would be to retreat and regroup."

"The smart thing would have been to stay home and pretend none of this was happening." She started moving toward the coordinates Rose had provided, power humming beneath her skin like a promise of violence. "But smart doesn't get answers, and answers are what we need."

Keats followed, because loyalty trumped common sense and because leaving her alone in enemy territory wasn't an option he could live with. But as they moved deeper into the Georgian wilderness, both of them carried the weight of what they'd become.

They were no longer the innocent teenagers who had started this journey seeking truth about divine heritage.

They were something else now, more dangerous, and infinitely more committed to seeing their mission through to its conclusion.

Whatever the cost.

CHAPTER 12: ALLIES AND ENEMIES

The abandoned Soviet radar installation materialized out of the mountain mist like a monument to paranoia and Cold War ambitions. Concrete structures jutted from the rocky landscape at impossible angles, their surfaces weathered by decades of alpine storms and neglect. However, what should have been a dead relic of twentieth-century conflict hummed with electronic activity and human presence.

Alexis crouched behind a boulder outcropping, studying the facility through binoculars while Keats monitored their surroundings for additional threats. The recent firefight had left them both hyperaware of potential ambushes, every shadow and sound evaluated as a possible threat.

"Three guard towers, rotating patrols, electronic surveillance equipment that definitely wasn't part of the original installation," she reported quietly. "Someone's put serious money into upgrading this place."

"Money and expertise," Keats added, pointing toward a communications array that bristled with satellite dishes and antenna systems. "That's military-grade gear, not surplus equipment."

Before Alexis could respond, a voice spoke from directly behind them. "You're right. And you're both about thirty seconds away from being very dead if you don't put those binoculars down and turn around slowly."

They froze, adrenaline spiking as the reality of their tactical mistake hit home. So focused on the facility, they'd failed to maintain proper perimeter awareness. Amateur mistake that could prove fatal.

"Easy," the voice continued. "I'm not with the people who just tried to kill you. But if you make any sudden movements, I might have to reconsider that position."

Alexis set down the binoculars and turned carefully, hands visible and empty. The man watching them looked like he'd stepped out of a Special Forces recruitment poster—mid-twenties, lean and dangerous, with the kind of controlled stillness that spoke of extensive combat experience. A wicked scar ran from his left temple to his jaw, and his pale blue eyes held the flat assessment of someone evaluating potential threats.

More significantly, he radiated the same supernatural pressure that marked divine heritage.

"Another Scion," she said, recognizing the familiar sensation of power recognizing power.

"Aaron Richardson," he replied, not lowering the assault rifle that was trained on her center mass. "Son of Ares, former U.S. Army Ranger, current pain in the ass to people who hunt our kind. And you're Alexis Rain, daughter of Nyx, currently wanted by approximately seventeen different organizations for reasons ranging from recruitment to immediate termination."

"You know who I am?"

"I make it my business to know every Scion who survives past their eighteenth birthday. There aren't many of us left." His expression remained neutral, but she caught the slight relaxation in his stance that suggested the conversation was proceeding better than he'd expected. "The question is whether you're here because you're working with the people in that facility, or because you're hunting them."

"Hunting," Keats said before Alexis could respond. "Definitely hunting. They killed her parents."

Aaron's rifle finally lowered, though he didn't sling it. "Then we have something in common. They've killed a lot of people I cared about too." He gestured toward the facility. "That installation is one of their primary research centers. They've been developing weapons specifically designed to neutralize Scions, testing them on subjects they've captured over the past few years."

"Testing them how?" Alexis asked, though she wasn't sure she wanted the answer.

"Vivisection. Psychological torture. Systematic documentation of our abilities and their limitations." Aaron's voice remained steady, but she caught the underlying current of rage that suggested personal experience with their methods. "The goal is to understand how divine blood interacts with human physiology so they can develop more effective ways to kill us."

The casual description of atrocities made Alexis's stomach clench with a mixture of nausea and fury. Bad enough that her parents had been murdered—the idea that other Scions were being tortured in the name of research added another layer of urgency to their mission.

"How many?" she asked.

"We estimate they've processed over forty subjects in the past two years. Most don't survive the initial experimentation phase." Aaron's expression grew grim. "The ones who do... well, they're not the same afterward. Broken in ways that don't heal."

"Jesus." Keats looked toward the facility with new understanding of what they'd stumbled into. "And nobody's tried to stop them?"

"Scions are hunted individuals, not an organized resistance movement. Most of us are too busy trying to survive to coordinate large-scale operations." Aaron slung his rifle across his back with practiced efficiency. "But that's changing. I've been building a network, gathering intelligence, preparing for the day when we can strike back effectively."

"What kind of network?"

"The kind that has satellite surveillance of facilities like this one, encrypted communication systems, and safe houses in major cities around the world." He started moving away from the installation, leading them toward a hidden position that offered better concealment. "The kind that's been tracking your movements since you left London and wondering whether you were an asset or a threat."

They followed him to a camouflaged observation post built into a natural cave system, where sophisticated monitoring equipment tracked activity at the facility in real-time. Inside, banks of screens showed feeds from cameras positioned throughout the installation, while communication intercepts provided real-time intelligence on guard rotations and operational schedules.

"This is impressive," Alexis said, studying the technical setup. "Military-grade surveillance and analysis capabilities. You didn't build this alone."

"No, I didn't. There are others—Scions who survived the culling, sympathetic mortals who understand what's at stake, even a few divine figures who've decided the old rules about non-interference need updating." Aaron settled at a control station, fingers dancing across keyboards with practiced efficiency. "But the enemy has resources too. Government backing, private funding, divine patronage from sources that prefer the old order to whatever we might represent."

"Divine patronage?"

"Some gods view Scions as aberrations that need to be eliminated. Others see us as tools to be controlled. Very few actually support our right to exist independently." He pulled up files on his primary monitor—organizational charts, financial records, operational summaries that painted a picture of coordinated persecution. "But there's someone pulling strings behind the scenes. Someone with enough power to coordinate supernatural assets while staying hidden from divine detection."

"Pitts," Alexis said, certainty crystallizing in her mind. "The man who killed my father. He's been orchestrating this."

Aaron's expression grew troubled. "Phthonos. Yes, we've been tracking his activities for months. Son of Nyx and Erebus, god of envy and resentment." Aaron glanced pointedly at Alexis. "Your half-brother."

The words hit her like physical blows. Half-brother. The stranger who had stalked her at Elizabeth's funeral, who had murdered Charles in cold blood, was family. Divine family, with the same cosmic heritage that flowed through her veins.

"He's been using mortal agents to do most of the actual killing," Aaron continued, oblivious to her emotional state. "Plausible deniability, you understand. Divine law technically forbids direct interference in mortal affairs, but there are loopholes if you're creative about interpretation."

"What kind of mortal agents?"

"Military contractors, intelligence operatives, true believers who think they're saving humanity from supernatural contamination." Aaron's jaw tightened. "Including some people who should know better. People who used to fight on our side."

"Meaning?"

Aaron went quiet for a long moment, staring at the surveillance photos.

"Harsh."

"You know him?"

"My brother." The words came out flat, empty. Aaron's hands clenched into fists. "Half-brother, technically. Same father, different mothers. We served together in Afghanistan."

Alexis waited, sensing there was more.

"He saved my life in Kandahar. I saved his in Helmand Province." Aaron's voice grew quieter. "Swore we'd always have each other's backs, no matter what. Then Phthonos got to him. Convinced him that people like us were... mistakes that needed correcting."

"Aaron, I'm sorry—"

"Don't." He turned away. "Just don't."

The personal betrayal in his words was devastating. Alexis understood now why Aaron had dedicated himself to building a resistance network, why he moved through the world with the controlled violence of someone who had lost everything that mattered and channeled that loss into purposeful action.

"Wait," Keats interjected. "If he is a Scion, why would he want to eliminate all Scions. That means he goes, too, right?"

"I'm not sure what kind of bullshit he's been fed. Along with the others. Whatever deal they've been promised, they're complete idiots to think that they won't eventually be on the hit list, as well." His eyes wandered from them to the depths of their hideout, as if remembering something.

"I'm sorry," Alexis said, meaning it.

"Don't be. Be angry. Be determined. Be ready to do whatever it takes to stop them." Aaron brought up another set of files—intelligence reports, surveillance photos, tactical assessments. "Because they're not going to stop with research and isolated killings. They're building toward something bigger. Something that could eliminate every Scion on the planet simultaneously."

"What do you mean?"

"We don't have all the details yet. But there are references in their communications to something called the Restoration Protocol. A final solution to what they consider the Scion problem." He highlighted specific intercepts, encrypted messages that had been partially decoded. "They're gathering artifacts, weapons of divine origin that could theoretically affect every person with mixed blood regardless of location."

The implications of that statement made Alexis's mouth go dry. Genocide on a cosmic scale, targeting everyone like her simply for existing. The systematic elimination of an entire category of beings because mortals found their existence threatening.

"How do we stop them?"

"First, we gather more intelligence. Find out exactly what they're planning and when they intend to implement it." Aaron stood, moving to a weapons locker that contained an impressive array of firearms and specialized ammunition. "But that's going to require taking significant risks. The kind of infiltration work that could get us all killed if we're not careful."

"What kind of infiltration work?"

"There's an Oracle in London. Carlos Mendez, son of Apollo, specializes in prophetic intelligence gathering. If anyone can provide insight into Phthonos's plans and timetables, it's him." Aaron selected a compact submachine gun and several magazines of the specialized ammunition they'd seen earlier. "But approaching him is dangerous. Oracles are valuable assets, which means they're heavily monitored by multiple factions."

"Monitored how?"

"Electronic surveillance, magical wards, protective details that include both mortal and supernatural elements." He handed Alexis a pistol designed for enhanced targets. "Plus, Carlos isn't entirely stable. Oracle abilities tend to fragment the psyche over time. He sees too many possible futures, gets confused about which timeline he's currently occupying."

Keats, who had been listening with growing unease, spoke up. "This is getting out of hand. We came here looking for information about how to find the one responsible for Charles's murder. Now we're talking about infiltrating London to consult with an insane Oracle about stopping cosmic genocide."

"The scope keeps expanding because the threat keeps expanding," Alexis replied, checking the pistol's action with movements that were becoming disturbingly natural. "We can't fight this piecemeal. If there really is a final solution in development, we need to understand it before it's too late to stop."

"At what cost?" Keats asked. "We've already killed six people today. How many more are we willing to sacrifice for information that might not even be accurate?"

The question hung in the air between them, loaded with implications about the people they were becoming and the prices they were willing to pay. Alexis understood his concern—the line between necessary violence and callous disregard for human life was thin and becoming thinner with each escalation.

But the alternative was accepting defeat and allowing Phthonos to proceed with whatever he was planning. That wasn't an option she could live with.

"As many as it takes," she said finally. "Because if we don't stop this, everyone like us dies. Everyone with divine blood, everyone who might someday have divine children, everyone who represents evolution beyond normal human limitations."

"And if we become monsters in the process of stopping monsters?"

"Then at least we'll be alive monsters." She met his gaze steadily. "I know you don't like where this is heading, Keats. I don't like it either. But I'm not going to let my parents' deaths be meaningless because I was too squeamish to do what needed to be done."

Aaron watched their argument with the detached interest of someone who had already fought similar battles with his own conscience. "For what it's worth," he said finally, "the people we're fighting don't share your moral qualms. They see us as a threat to be eliminated, not fellow beings deserving of ethical consideration. Restraint is a luxury we can't afford if we want to survive."

"Survival isn't the only thing that matters," Keats insisted. "Staying human matters too."

"Does it?" Alexis turned to face him fully, power beginning to stir beneath her skin. "Because I'm not human, Keats. I'm something else, something that scares mortals enough that they're willing to commit genocide to eliminate the threat we represent. Maybe it's time I stopped pretending otherwise."

The words created a schism between them that felt like physical distance despite their proximity. For the first time since childhood, they were looking at the same situation and reaching fundamentally different conclusions about the appropriate response.

"So what happens next?" Keats asked. "We go to London, we consult with the Oracle, we gather intelligence about this Restoration Protocol. And then what? We declare war on every organization that's hunting Scions? We become the very thing they're afraid we'll become?"

"Maybe," Alexis said. "Or maybe we find a way to stop them without losing ourselves in the process. But either way, we move forward. Because standing still means dying slowly while they pick us off one by one."

Aaron cleared his throat, drawing their attention back to immediate tactical concerns. "Actually, there's something else you should know before you make any decisions about London. Something that changes the risk assessment significantly."

"What?"

"Carlos isn't just any Oracle. He's one of the most powerful prophetic talents we've identified. Which means consulting with him will send ripples through the supernatural community that every major player will notice." Aaron's expression grew grim. "The moment you make contact with him, everyone hunting you will know exactly where you are and what you're trying to accomplish."

"A trap," Keats said with bitter satisfaction. "I told you this was getting out of hand."

"Not a trap," Alexis corrected. "An opportunity. If everyone hunting us converges on London, then we'll finally have a chance to confront them directly instead of constantly reacting to their moves."

"If everyone…" Keats stared at his best friend as if she had two heads. "You want to jump blindly into a situation where you don't know who your enemies are or how many there may be. Just jump into battle unprepared? Al, we're still just kids. We aren't soldiers." He glanced quickly at Aaron who shrugged acquiescence.

"Then we'd better make sure we're ready for it." She turned back to Aaron. "I can get us to London."

"Transportation's not the issue. Preparation is. To Keats' point." He moved to another equipment locker, this one containing items that radiated subtle supernatural energies. "If you're really going to do this, you'll need more than conventional weapons and good intentions. You'll need tools designed specifically for supernatural warfare."

As Aaron began outlining the resources available to them, Alexis felt the weight of the decision she was making. They were crossing another threshold, moving from reactive survival to proactive engagement with forces that had been hunting their kind for Zeus knew how long.

Alexis lost herself in thought for a moment. It seemed the innocent teenagers who had started this journey seeking answers about divine heritage were gone, replaced by something tougher and more dangerous. Something that understood the true cost of the war they were fighting and was prepared to pay that cost.

Whatever it took to ensure their enemies paid a higher one.

But as she met Keats's troubled gaze across the weapons cache, Alexis wondered if survival would be worth the price of what they were becoming.

The question would have to wait for an answer.

Right now, there were battles to plan and enemies to hunt.

The war for the future of their kind was about to begin in earnest.

CHAPTER 13: VISIONS AND REVELATIONS

The abandoned church in East London squatted between derelict row houses like a broken tooth in a diseased mouth. Gothic arches reached toward overcast skies with fingers of crumbling stone, while stained glass windows wept colored light onto streets that had forgotten the meaning of sanctuary. It was exactly the kind of place an unstable Oracle would choose for a meeting—isolated, atmospheric, and removed from the surveillance networks that monitored more conventional locations.

They had arrived twenty minutes ago, began scouting the area. Aaron's intelligence stated that Carlos would be here. He just didn't know when. Or, if he would have any contact with Alexis and Keats, at all. This was nothing if not a fluid situation.

Alexis stood in the shadow of a construction crane, studying the building through binoculars while Keats monitored their approach routes. Three days had passed since their encounter with Aaron Richardson in the Caucasus Mountains, three days of surveilling, training, learning through increasingly dangerous methods while their argument festered like an infected wound.

"Still think this is a mistake," Keats said, his voice carrying the flat tone he'd adopted, now, whenever discussing their mission. "We're walking into another trap, just like the mountains."

"Everything's a trap now." Alexis lowered the binoculars, frustration bleeding through her carefully maintained composure. "The question is whether we let that stop us from gathering the intelligence we need."

"Intelligence gathered from an Oracle who may or may not be completely insane."

"As opposed to what? Sitting in safe houses while Pitts picks off every Scion on the planet one by one? Or, worse, wipes us out all at once?" She turned to face him, noting the way he flinched slightly from the anger in her voice. "We need prophetic guidance, Keats. Carlos Mendez is the only Oracle Aaron's network has identified who's both powerful enough and stable enough to provide useful information."

"Stable being a relative term."

"Everything's relative when you're dealing with cosmic forces." She had spent a lot of time in her own head of late. Asking question after question. Extending her access to knowledge as far as she could. Now, faced with all of the knowledge she obtained, Alexis couldn't help but feel more than a little overwhelmed. She would not, however, let that show. Especially not to Keats, who could usually read her like a book. She started moving toward the church, weapons checking against her ribs with each step. "The question is whether you're coming with me or staying here to provide overwatch."

"You know I'm not letting you go in there alone."

The words should have been comforting, but they carried an undercurrent of resentment that made them feel more like an obligation than a choice. Their relationship had been strained since the firefight in the mountains, each of them processing the violence differently and reaching incompatible conclusions about what it meant for their future.

Keats saw the killing as a necessary evil that threatened to consume their humanity if they weren't careful. Alexis saw it as the price of survival in a war that had been declared on them by forces beyond their control.

The difference in perspective was becoming a chasm that threatened to swallow their friendship entirely. For Alexis, that was what was most troubling. As she'd been lost in her head, trying to open herself up to as much knowledge and understanding as she could, it was inevitable that Keats didn't slip in there somewhere. She'd been pondering their relationship. Their friendship. Their near-familial bond. She'd come to a conclusion but it wasn't anything she wanted to share. Not yet. Not when they were likely fighting for their lives and lives of so many others.

They approached the church through a maze of construction equipment and abandoned vehicles, using cover and concealment techniques Aaron had drilled into them during their brief training sessions. The building's interior was a study in elegant decay—pews arranged in perfect rows despite their rotting wood, an altar that still held the remnants of recent offerings, stone columns that had weathered centuries of prayers and disappointments.

Carlos Mendez sat in the front pew with his back to the entrance, a slight figure in an expensive suit that looked incongruous against the derelict surroundings. His dark hair was shot through with premature silver, and when he turned to greet them, Alexis saw eyes that held the fractured intensity of someone who lived in multiple timelines simultaneously.

"Alexis Rain," he said, his voice carrying a slight Spanish accent colored by years of living in various countries. "Daughter of Nyx, seeker of truths that would be better left buried. And Jamie Keats, son of light and prophecy, though he doesn't know it yet."

The casual revelation about Keats's parentage hit like a physical blow. Alexis felt her friend go rigid beside her, his breathing becoming shallow and controlled in the way that suggested emotional shock.

"What did you just say?" Keats asked.

"That you're more than you know. More than either of you know." Carlos gestured for them to sit, his movements carrying the careful precision of someone navigating multiple realities. "But we'll come to that. First, let me share what I've seen about the path you're walking."

He closed his eyes, and the air around him began to shimmer with the same heat distortion Alexis associated with divine power. When he spoke again, his voice carried the resonant authority of prophecy itself.

"I see fire and shadow, cosmic forces in conflict across multiple dimensions. I see the daughter of night standing at the center of a maelstrom that could unmake reality itself, choosing between salvation and destruction while the universe holds its breath."

Images flashed through Alexis's mind—visions that felt more real than memory, glimpses of possible futures where she stood wreathed in power that could reshape existence with a thought. In some, she was a protector, using her abilities to shield the innocent from cosmic predators. In others, she was something else entirely, a force of pure destruction that left nothing but ashes in her wake.

"I see the Book of Fates," Carlos continued, his voice growing stronger as the prophecy built momentum. "The most dangerous artifact in existence, containing the fundamental laws that govern reality itself. Written by the Moirai before time had meaning, it holds the power to rewrite the basic structure of the universe."

"What does that have to do with us?" Alexis asked, though part of her already knew the answer.

"Everything. Because your brother—Phthonos, god of envy—has found a way to access it. And he intends to use it to erase every Scion from existence, retroactively removing divine-mortal hybrids from the timeline itself."

The implications of that statement made the church seem to spin around her. Not just genocide of existing Scions, but cosmic revision that would ensure they had never existed at all. The elimination of an entire category of beings from the fundamental structure of reality.

"That's impossible," Keats said. "No one has that kind of power."

"No one except someone with the ability to read and interpret the Book of Fates." Carlos opened his eyes, focusing on Keats with laser intensity. "Which brings us to you, young Oracle. Son of Apollo, god of prophecy and light. Son of Cassandra, the legendary Oracle of Troy whose gift was to see true futures but never be believed."

The revelation hit Keats like a sledgehammer. He went pale, swaying slightly as the full weight of his divine heritage crashed down on him. "That's... that's not possible. My mother is Katy Keats, a nurse at Mount Pleasant General Hospital."

"Your mother, yes," Carlos's expression softened slightly. "Cassandra chose to live as a mortal after the fall of Troy, hiding her identity and raising her son in the protection of anonymity. But divine blood will tell, eventually. Your unusual insights, your ability to anticipate Alexis's needs, your survival of situations that should have killed you—all evidence of your true heritage."

"Why does it matter? His heritage. What are you getting at?" Alexis asked, though she was beginning to understand the cosmic significance of Keats's parentage.

"It matters because the combination of Apollo's prophetic power and Cassandra's gift for seeing true futures makes him the only being in existence capable of reading the Book of Fates accurately. Phthonos needs him to access the book's power, which is why he's been maneuvering events to bring you both within his reach."

The statement hung in the air like a loaded weapon, transforming their entire journey from a quest for answers into an elaborate trap designed to capture the one person who could help Pitts rewrite reality itself.

"He's been herding us," Alexis said, pieces falling into place with terrifying clarity. "Every clue, every lead, every encounter designed to push us toward this moment."

"Not herding. Hunting. But the prey he really wants isn't you—it's Jamie." Carlos stood, his prophecy apparently complete. "Which means your friend is in more danger than you know."

As if summoned by his words, the church's windows exploded inward in a shower of multicolored glass. Dark figures poured through the openings with inhuman speed, moving with the coordinated precision of a military assault team augmented by supernatural abilities.

"Contact!" Keats shouted, diving behind a pew as gunfire erupted across the sanctuary.

But these weren't ordinary soldiers. They moved too fast, absorbed too much damage, displayed reflexes that spoke of divine enhancement. Alexis accessed the ether, stepping between dimensions to appear behind the nearest attacker, but found her path blocked by some kind of mystical barrier that made dimensional transit feel like pushing through molasses.

"Warded," Carlos called out, taking cover behind the altar. "The entire building is locked down against supernatural abilities. We're trapped."

Alexis drew her pistol and returned fire, but she could already see the tactical situation deteriorating. Too many attackers, too little cover, and no way to use her primary advantage against enemies who had clearly prepared for her abilities.

The engagement lasted less than three minutes. When the smoke cleared, Carlos lay unconscious behind the altar, Alexis knelt bleeding from a dozen minor wounds, and Keats was gone.

"JAMIE!" she screamed, power building beneath her skin despite the mystical interference. Silver light began pouring from her in waves that made the air itself vibrate with potential energy.

But it was too late. The attackers had vanished as quickly as they'd appeared, taking Keats with them and leaving only the smell of ozone and the echo of supernatural ferocity.

Carlos stirred, struggling to sit up against the altar. Blood ran from his nose and ears, evidence of the psychic backlash that came from having a prophecy interrupted by violence.

"Gone," he whispered, his voice barely audible. "Taken to the place where shadows gather and envy feeds on cosmic power. The old one has what he came for."

"Where?" Alexis demanded, kneeling beside him. "Where did they take him?"

"I see... a place of learning. Ancient knowledge preserved in towers of glass and steel. But not the knowledge mortals think they've stored there." Carlos's eyes rolled back, showing only whites as another vision took hold. "The fiery one waits in mountains of granite and snow. Daughter of speed and messages, guardian of those who share our burden. Find her. She alone can teach you what you need to know."

"What do I need to know?"

"How to burn the world and build it anew. How to choose between love and justice when both paths lead to damnation." His voice grew fainter, more distant. "The White Mountains. New Hampshire. Where the children of gods learn to survive in a world that wants them dead."

He slumped forward, unconscious but breathing. Alexis checked his pulse—

steady but weak—then stood and surveyed the wreckage of the church. Bullet holes in ancient stone, broken glass scattered like fallen stars, the lingering scent of supernatural power and human violence.

Keats was gone. Taken by enemies who intended to use him as a key to unlock cosmic forces that could unravel reality itself. And she was alone, standing in the ruins of another trap with nothing but Carlos's cryptic prophecy to guide her next move.

The White Mountains. The fiery one. Someone who could teach her what she needed to know to save Keats and stop Pitts from rewriting the fundamental structure of existence.

It wasn't much of a plan, but it was all she had.

As she stepped carefully through the broken glass toward the church's exit, Alexis felt something fundamental shift in her understanding of the conflict she was fighting. This wasn't just about hunting the people who had killed her parents or protecting other Scions from systematic persecution.

This was about the survival of reality itself.

And somewhere in the darkness, her best friend was being prepared for a role that would either save the universe or destroy it completely.

The question was whether she could reach him in time to make sure it was the former rather than the latter.

CHAPTER 14: PROPHECY AND PERIL

Alexis stood in the wreckage of the church, Carlos's words echoing in her mind like the tolling of funeral bells. Keats—taken, gone, in the hands of enemies who needed him for something that could unmake the very fabric of reality. The Book of Fates. The power to rewrite existence itself. And her best friend as the only key that could unlock that cosmic weapon.

She knelt beside Carlos, who was stirring weakly against the altar, blood still trickling from his nose where the interrupted prophecy had backlashed through his nervous system. His eyes fluttered open, focusing on her with effort.

"How long?" she asked.

"Days. Maybe a week. Time moves differently when the Fates themselves are involved." His voice was hoarse, damaged by the violence that had torn through his prophetic vision. "But not long enough. Never long enough when the universe itself hangs in the balance."

"Tell me about the Book. Everything you know."

Carlos struggled to sit up straighter, his movements careful and deliberate. "Written by the Moirai before the first stars ignited. Contains the fundamental algorithms that govern reality—the laws of physics, the progression of time, the boundaries between life and death. Most beings can't even look at it without going insane. Those who can read it..."

"Can rewrite those laws?"

"Can rewrite everything." He met her gaze with eyes that held the weight of cosmic knowledge. "Imagine being able to edit the basic code of existence. Remove the law of gravity, reverse the flow of time, decide that certain types of beings never existed in the first place. That's what Phthonos is trying to accomplish."

The scope of the threat made her feel dizzy. Not just the death of existing Scions, but their complete erasure from the timeline. Everyone like her, everyone who might someday be like her, simply... gone. As if they had never been.

"And Jamie can read it because of his parentage?"

"Apollo's prophetic sight combined with Cassandra's gift for seeing true futures. No other combination of divine heritage could penetrate the Book's defenses. He hasn't realized his own potential. Far from it. And, Phthonos is going to force that realization to the point Keats can then understand the Book." Carlos closed his eyes, accessing memories that might have been his own or borrowed from other oracles. "Phthonos has been planning this for centuries, waiting for someone with the right bloodline to be born. When your friend manifested his abilities, it set everything in motion."

"Manifested? When?" Alexis was trying to understand but her brain felt like it was on fire. So much all at once. She was struggling to put all the pieces together properly.

"Carlos closed his eyes, even as he used the sleeve of his suit to wipe the blood away from his nose. "When you were sparring. In the class. He has been relying on his prophetic abilities without even realizing it. That was the alarm that Phthonos was waiting for."

"Then why take him now? Why not wait until he was fully trained?"

"Because you were becoming too dangerous. Your power is growing exponentially, and soon you'll be strong enough to challenge him directly. He needed to move before you realized your full potential." Carlos's expression grew troubled. "Plus, there's something else. Something I saw in the final moments of my vision before the attack."

"What?"

"Jamie isn't just the key to reading the Book of Fates. He's also the only thing that can stop Phthonos from using it." Carlos gripped her arm with surprising strength. "The Oracle's curse. Passed down from Cassandra herself. True prophecy that's never believed. If Jamie can speak the words that would prevent the rewriting of reality, but do it in a way that Phthonos doesn't believe them..."

"He could trick him into making the wrong choice."

"Potentially. But it would require perfect timing, complete understanding of the Book's mechanisms, and the kind of courage that comes from knowing you're probably going to die in the attempt." Carlos released her arm. "Which is why you need to find the fiery one. She can teach you things that no one else knows, prepare you for a confrontation that will determine the fate of everything."

"Who is she?"

"Lily Abrams. Daughter of Hermes, master of speed and communication, guardian of those the world has forgotten. She's been building a network to protect Scions, keeping them hidden from the forces that hunt our kind." His voice grew weaker, the strain of prophecy and violence taking its toll. "But more than that, she understands something that most of our kind never learn—how to use divine power without losing your humanity in the process."

"Where in the White Mountains?"

"I see... granite peaks and snow-fed streams. A place where children learn to harness lightning and walk through walls. Where the old gods' children gather to remember what they are and choose what they want to become." Carlos slumped back against the altar, exhausted. "Find the cave that was never meant to be found. She'll be waiting."

Alexis stood, decision crystallizing in her mind. "How much time do I have?"

"Like I said, a few days. Maybe a week if we're fortunate. The Book of Fates isn't easily accessed, even by someone with the right heritage. Phthonos will need time to prepare Jamie, to break down his resistance and ensure compliance." His expression grew grim. "But once he begins the rewriting process, there will be no stopping it. Reality itself will bend to his will."

"Then I'd better get moving."

She turned to leave, but Carlos's voice stopped her at the broken doorway. "Alexis. There's something else you need to understand about the path you're walking."

"What?"

"The power you'll need to stop Phthonos... it will change you. Transform you into something that's no longer entirely mortal, no longer entirely sane by conventional standards. The daughter of Nyx who can challenge a god directly isn't the same person who cried at her father's funeral."

"Will I still be me?"

"That depends on what you consider to be the essential parts of yourself. Your memories will remain, your core personality will survive. But your perspective on existence itself will be... altered. You'll see the universe as it truly is, not as mortals perceive it." Carlos's voice carried the weight of personal experience with transformation. "The question you need to ask yourself is whether saving Jamie and stopping the rewriting of reality is worth becoming something that can never go back to being human."

The question hung in the air between them, loaded with implications about sacrifice and the prices that came with cosmic power. Alexis thought about Keats, probably terrified and alone in whatever mystical prison Pitts had prepared for him. About the systematic elimination of everyone like her, the genocidal ambitions of a divine being who saw Scions as aberrations to be erased.

About the choice between remaining human and becoming something capable of protecting the people she loved.

"Yes," she said finally. "It's worth it. And, I will always be human. I am my father's daughter as much as I may be Nyx's. That will never change. But, I will do whatever it takes to save Keats and all of the Scions, if I can."

"Then may the gods have mercy on us all." Carlos closed his eyes, his part in events complete. "Because once you choose that path, there's no turning back. You'll become something unprecedented—a primordial force walking in mortal flesh, wielding power that could remake the cosmos itself."

"Or destroy it completely?"

"That too."

Alexis left Carlos there in the ruins of the church, surrounded by broken glass and the lingering scent of supernatural violence. Outside, London continued its daily routine—millions of people going about their lives, completely unaware that the fundamental structure of reality hung in the balance.

As she walked through the crowded streets toward the nearest transportation hub, her mind raced through the logistics of reaching New Hampshire. Commercial flight would be fastest but also most monitored. The ether was still partially blocked by whatever mystical interference had trapped them in the church. Which left conventional travel and the growing certainty that every moment of delay brought Jamie closer to a fate worse than death.

Behind her, shadows lengthened despite the afternoon sun, and in those shadows something vast and patient began to stir. The daughter of Nyx was finally embracing her destiny.

And, cosmic forces were taking notice.

CHAPTER 15: THE FIERY ONE

The White Mountains of New Hampshire stretched across Alexis's vision like a granite fortress, ancient peaks rising into the early summer sky while dense forests of pine and birch created a green carpet that rolled away to the horizon. She stood on the edge of the ether, studying the terrain below while trying to identify whatever sanctuary Carlos had mentioned in his prophecy.

Two days had passed since Keats's kidnapping, two days of traveling across an ocean while her abilities grew stronger and her control grew more tenuous. She took every opportunity for solitude so that she could practice her abilities, strengthen her control as much as possible. Still, she could feel the seeds of a growing power, essence, that longed to be set free. Dimensional transit had also become easier—almost effortless—but the power building beneath her skin felt like carrying a nuclear reactor around that could detonate at any moment.

She stepped out of the ether into a grove of towering pine trees, materializing in a shaft of afternoon sunlight that filtered through the canopy in golden columns. The air was warm and fragrant with the scents of pine resin and wildflowers, carrying the promise of a New England summer at its peak.

The arrow took her in the left shoulder before she'd been in normal reality for three full seconds.

The impact spun her around and sent her stumbling against a moss-covered boulder, silver fire exploding from her skin in an automatic defensive response. Pain blazed through her nervous system—not just the physical trauma of the arrow, but some kind of mystical burning that suggested the projectile wasn't entirely conventional.

"Ow!" a cheerful voice called from somewhere above her. "That looked like it hurt. You might want to stay down until we figure out whether you're a friendly visitor or another assassin sent to ruin my day." The voice was high enough to be female and was carried along by a weird sing-song cadence.

Alexis pressed her back against the boulder, power building toward a violent release while she searched for the source of the voice. The arrow had punched clean through her shoulder, leaving a wound that bled freely despite her enhanced healing. Whatever the projectile was made of, it was designed to penetrate supernatural defenses.

"I'm not an assassin," she called back, trying to project calm while divine energy crackled around her like contained lightning. "Carlos Mendez sent me. I'm looking for Lily Abrams."

"Oh good! That means you're probably not here to kill me." A figure dropped from the branches of a massive pine tree with fluid grace, landing on the forest floor without making a sound. "Though I have to say, materializing out of thin air in someone's territory is generally considered poor etiquette."

Lily Abrams looked like she'd stepped out of a mythology textbook's illustration of divine messengers. Medium height with a lean, athletic build that spoke of constant movement, vibrant red hair that seemed to glow with its own inner fire, and bright green eyes that sparkled with mischief and intelligence. She wore practical hiking gear—boots, cargo pants, and a tank top that revealed toned arms etched with small scars—but moved with the fluid grace that marked divine heritage.

"You tried to kill me," Alexis pointed out, noting the way Lily held a compound bow with the casual competence of someone who had been using weapons since childhood.

"No, dummy. I just shot you. If I'd been trying to kill you, the arrow would have gone through your heart instead of your shoulder." Lily approached with the confidence of someone operating on home turf. "Besides, it's not like it's going to kill you. You're a Scion, right? Daughter of someone cosmically significant? You'll heal."

"It's not healing."

"Because the arrow's still in there, obviously. I'd say that's better removed, yeah? Divine-forged steel disrupts supernatural healing until it's removed." Lily gestured toward the shaft protruding from Alexis's shoulder. "Think of it as a mystical splinter. Very painful, completely non-fatal, easily fixed once you learn the right technique."

"What technique?"

"Channel your divine energy into restoration instead of destruction. Your power wants to fix you—it's designed to maintain the vessel that carries it. You just need to stop thinking of it as a weapon and start thinking of it as a tool."

The suggestion ran counter to every instinct Alexis had developed since her abilities first manifested. For weeks, she'd been using her power as a defensive system, something that protected her by destroying threats. The idea of turning that same energy inward felt dangerous, like pointing a loaded gun at her own chest.

But the arrow was making it difficult to focus, and the mystical burning was spreading through her nervous system like infection. If Lily was right about the disruption effect, the wound would only get worse until the foreign object was removed.

"How?" she asked.

"Close your eyes. Feel the power moving through you—not the destructive aspects, but the life force itself. Divine energy is fundamentally creative, not destructive. It builds stars, shapes planets, creates the conditions for life to flourish." Lily's voice took on the cadence of instruction, suggesting she'd taught this lesson before. "Now reach for that creative aspect and direct it toward your shoulder."

Alexis closed her eyes and tried to sense the silver fire that had been her constant companion since Elizabeth's death. Instead of the weapon she'd learned to wield, she searched for something deeper—the cosmic force that had shaped her from conception, that maintained her existence despite the incompatible mixture of divine and mortal heritage.

There. A warm current that felt like starlight made manifest, flowing through channels she hadn't known existed. She guided it toward the wound, visualizing restoration instead of destruction, healing instead of harm.

The arrow dissolved, its mystical components breaking down under the influence of directed divine energy. The wound closed with a sensation like warm honey flowing through damaged tissue, leaving behind only slightly marked skin and the memory of pain.

"Well done," Lily said approvingly. "Most Scions take weeks to learn that trick. You figured it out in minutes."

"I had good motivation." Alexis opened her eyes, testing the mobility of her shoulder. Perfect function, no residual damage, not even a scar to mark where the arrow had been. "Why did you shoot me?"

"Because showing up unannounced in someone's sanctuary is a good way to get yourself killed, and I wanted to make sure you understood that before we started sharing sensitive information." Lily slung her bow across her back with practiced efficiency. "Plus, you needed to learn the healing technique. You'll need it where you're going."

"Which is where?"

"Into the kind of conflict that gets people shot with much worse things than practice arrows." Lily started walking deeper into the forest, her movements sure and confident despite the lack of visible paths. "But first, let me show you what I've built here. I think you'll find it educational."

They hiked through pine forests and across babbling streams, following what appeared to be game trails that wound between massive granite boulders and stands of ancient trees. The late afternoon air was warm and humid, filled with the sounds of birds and insects that spoke of wilderness undisturbed by human presence.

"How many people know about this place?" she asked.

"Depends on what you mean by people. Normal humans? Zero. Government agencies? Maybe three or four individuals with high enough clearance and open enough minds to process supernatural intelligence. Other Scions?" Lily grinned. "Let's just say we're not the only ones who've figured out that hiding in plain sight is the best way to avoid becoming extinct."

They climbed steadily upward, following what appeared to be a deer path that wound between the granite outcroppings and stands of birch trees. The terrain grew more rugged as they gained elevation, but Lily moved with the tireless efficiency of someone accustomed to mountain hiking.

"There," she said, pointing toward what looked like a solid rock face stretching up the mountainside. "Home sweet home."

Alexis studied the granite wall, noting subtle irregularities in the stone that suggested artificial modification. "I don't see anything."

"That's the point." Lily approached the rock face and pressed her palm against what appeared to be solid stone. The surface shimmered like heat mirage, revealing an opening large enough for a person to pass through. "Mystical camouflage. Looks like natural rock formation to anyone who doesn't know the access key."

They stepped through the hidden entrance into a cave system that defied every expectation Alexis had formed about underground spaces. Instead of cramped tunnels and dripping stalactites, she found herself in a vast natural chamber lit by some kind of ambient illumination that seemed to come from the stone itself.

"Welcome to our command center," Lily announced, gesturing toward a sophisticated installation that would have made Aaron Richardson's mountain facility look primitive by comparison. "Carved out of solid granite by some very patient Scions with earth-moving abilities, powered by geothermal energy and shielded from electronic surveillance by about three hundred feet of mountain."

The cave complex stretched deeper into the mountain than Alexis could see, with multiple chambers branching off from the main space. Banks of monitors displayed real-time intelligence feeds from around the world, while sophisticated encryption equipment handled secure communications between network nodes.

"This is impressive," she said, studying tactical displays that tracked Scion movements and threat assessments across multiple continents. "How long have you been building this?"

"Six years, since my mother was killed by Hough's people and I decided that hiding wasn't enough anymore." Lily settled at a control station, fingers dancing across keyboards with practiced efficiency. "Started with just me and a laptop in a tent, trying to warn other Scions about the hunting teams. Grew from there as more survivors found their way to us."

"And the government doesn't know about this?"

"Oh, they know something's here. Hard to hide this level of organization from satellite surveillance and electronic intelligence gathering." Lily pulled up classified documents that made Alexis's eyes widen. "But we've got allies in the right places, people who understand that not all supernatural threats need to be eliminated. Plus, we're careful to present ourselves as a monitoring service rather than a resistance movement."

"But you are a resistance movement."

"Absolutely. We just prefer to think of ourselves as a humanitarian organization that happens to be really good at making problems disappear." Lily's grin turned sharp and dangerous. "Speaking of which, we know about your friend. Jamie Keats, son of Apollo and Cassandra, currently being held by Phthonos in a facility designed to extract prophetic compliance through psychological manipulation."

The casual delivery of information Alexis desperately needed made her sink into the nearest chair. "You know where he is?"

"We know where he was as of eighteen hours ago. Phthonos moves his operations frequently, but he can't completely hide the mystical signatures involved in containing an Oracle of Jamie's potential. Once we figured out what we were trying to track, it was simple enough to attune our equipment to look for... well, one of the most powerful Oracles to ever be born."

Alexis tried to wrap her head around that. All this time, she had felt as if Keats were there to keep an eye out for her, to help keep her safe. Turns out she had failed miserably at that same task.

Lily brought up surveillance imagery that showed a modern office building in what looked like Manhattan. "But before we talk about rescue operations, you need to understand what you're really walking into."

"What do you mean?"

"I mean this isn't just about saving your friend, though that's obviously important. This is about preventing the systematic rewriting of universal law." Lily pulled up files that made Alexis's blood run cold—technical specifications for mystical devices, theoretical papers on temporal manipulation, intelligence reports about artifact acquisitions. "Carlos sent us the details. Phthonos has been gathering components for something called the Restoration Protocol. A way to eliminate every Scion from existence retroactively."

"Carlos mentioned something called the Book of Fates."

"The keystone of the whole operation. Contains the fundamental algorithms that govern reality itself. And your friend is the only person alive who can read it accurately enough for Phthonos to use it." Lily's expression grew grim. "Which means we can't just charge in guns blazing. We need intelligence first, a clear understanding of his defenses and timeline."

"What kind of intelligence?"

"The kind that requires someone with your abilities to get close enough to his facility for reconnaissance without triggering every alarm he's got installed." Lily stood, moving to a weapons locker carved directly into the granite wall. "But that means you need training first. Real training, not the trial-by-fire education you've been getting."

"What kind of training?"

"How to use your powers with precision instead of just raw force. How to shield yourself from detection by hostile mystical sensors. How to gather intelligence without getting caught, captured, or killed." Lily pulled out equipment that radiated subtle supernatural energies. "The basics of staying alive when you're operating in enemy territory."

"How long will that take?"

"Depends on how fast you learn. Most Scions need weeks to develop proper control and stealth techniques." Lily assessed her with professional interest. "But you're not most Scions, are you? Daughter of Nyx, stable power development, combat experience under pressure. I'm thinking we can get you ready in forty-eight hours if you're willing to push yourself."

"And then?"

"Then you infiltrate Phthonos's facility, gather intelligence on his defenses and timeline, and get out without anyone knowing you were there." Lily's smile was fierce and bright with anticipation. "Think of it as the final exam for Advanced Supernatural Warfare."

Alexis thought about Keats, probably terrified and alone in whatever mystical prison Pitts had prepared for him. About the systematic elimination of everyone like her, the genocidal ambitions of a divine being who saw Scions as aberrations to be erased from existence itself.

"When do we start?" she asked.

"Right now." Lily moved to a section of the cave that had been cleared of equipment, providing space for training exercises. "Because every hour we delay is another hour closer to the moment when your friend becomes the key to unmaking reality itself."

As they began working through the fundamentals of controlled power application, Alexis felt the weight of cosmic responsibility settling on her shoulders. She was no longer just trying to save her best friend or get revenge for her parents' deaths.

She was preparing to prevent the literal end of everything Scion.

And somewhere in the depths of her divine heritage, ancient powers were stirring in response to her growing determination.

The daughter of Nyx was finally learning to claim her birthright.

She only hoped she would master it in time to save the universe from her own brother's envy.

CHAPTER 16: DIVINE POLITICS

The morning sun streamed through the cave entrance with an intensity that seemed to fill the granite chamber with liquid gold. Alexis had been practicing stealth techniques for six hours straight, learning to dampen her divine signature while maintaining enough power to access her abilities at a moment's notice. Her muscles ached from the precision work, but her control had improved dramatically under Lily's relentless instruction.

"Better," Lily said, studying the mystical sensors that monitored Alexis's energy output. "You're down to background radiation levels. Most supernatural detection systems would read you as a normal human with maybe some latent psychic potential."

"It feels like holding my breath underwater," Alexis replied, maintaining the careful mental discipline required to keep her power contained. "How long can I sustain this?"

"With practice? Hours. Maybe days if you're willing to accept some discomfort." Lily shut down the monitoring equipment. "But we're not done yet. You need to understand how the broader network operates before you go into hostile territory."

She led Alexis deeper into the cave system, past chambers filled with communication equipment and storage areas that contained enough supplies to sustain a small army. The operation was more extensive than Alexis had realized—not just a command center, but a fully functional underground base capable of supporting long-term resistance operations.

"Impressive setup, yes?" a male voice said from behind them. "Though I have to question the operational security of discussing sensitive information where anyone could walk in unannounced."

Alexis spun around, power spiking toward combat readiness before Lily's hand on her arm stopped her from launching an attack. The man standing in the cave entrance looked like he'd stepped out of a magazine advertisement for expensive outdoor gear— mid-thirties, perfectly groomed dark hair, and a smile that could have sold a million products. But underneath the surface charm, she felt the unmistakable pressure of divine power.

"Relax," Lily said, though her own posture suggested she was anything but relaxed. "Alex, meet Alexis Rain. Alexis, this is Alex Delphi. He's... a consultant."

"A consultant," Alexis repeated, studying the newcomer with the wariness that had kept her alive this long. "What kind of consultant?"

"The kind who's been breaking cosmic law for the past several years by providing aid and assistance to Scions." Alex's smile widened, revealing teeth that were too perfect and eyes that held depths no mortal gaze could achieve. "Though I prefer to think of it as providing strategic guidance to talented young people who happen to need it."

The formal phrasing and casual admission of lawbreaking told Alexis everything she needed to know about his true identity. "You're a god."

"Guilty as charged." The illusion of mortality fell away like a discarded coat, revealing the full weight of his divine presence. Light began to emanate from his skin, not the harsh glare of electrical illumination but the warm radiance of summer sunlight. "Apollo, if you want to use the traditional name. God of light, prophecy, healing, and music. Also, incidentally, Jamie's father."

The revelation hit Alexis like a physical blow. She'd known intellectually that Keats had divine parentage, but meeting his actual father transformed abstract knowledge into visceral reality. This being—ancient, powerful, operating on a cosmic scale she could barely comprehend—had been watching his son from a distance for eighteen years.

"Where were you?" The question came out harder than she'd intended, carrying all the accumulated anger and grief of the past few weeks. "When he needed you, when people were hunting him, when Pitts kidnapped him—where the hell were you?"

Apollo's radiance dimmed slightly, his expression shifting from casual charm to something that might have been regret. "Bound by laws older than human civilization. Divine intervention in mortal affairs is strictly regulated, monitored by forces that make the most oppressive government surveillance look primitive by comparison."

"But you're here now."

"Because the situation has escalated beyond normal parameters. When one of our own—Phthonos—begins actively hunting Scions with the intent of erasing them from existence, the old restrictions become... flexible." He moved deeper into the cave, his presence making the air itself seem to vibrate with potential energy. "Though I should mention that my being here represents a significant political risk."

"Political how?"

"The Olympian Council is divided on the Scion question. Some view you as evolutionary progress, the next step in the development of both divine and mortal species. Others see you as dangerous aberrations, born of bored gods, that threaten cosmic stability." Apollo settled onto a small granite ledge that had been carved into a makeshift bench. "My involvement with Scion protection efforts has not gone unnoticed."

Lily moved to her communication station, pulling up files that showed the scope of their intelligence operations. "Alex has been our primary source for information about divine politics and supernatural threats that originate above the mortal level."

"At considerable personal cost," Apollo added. "If certain members of the Council discover the extent of my assistance, I could face censure, imprisonment, or worse."

"Then why risk it?"

"Because Jamie is my son. Because you and others like you represent something unprecedented and precious. And because I've seen what happens when gods allow fear to override wisdom." His expression grew troubled. "The Titans were destroyed not because they were evil, but because they represented change that the younger gods couldn't control. I won't allow history to repeat itself with Scions."

The comparison to the Titans sent ice through Alexis's veins. The idea that gods might view her kind as a threat requiring elimination on the same scale as the cosmic war that had reshaped the universe itself.

"How many others?" she asked. "How many gods are involved in either protecting or hunting Scions?"

"Fewer than you might hope, more than we can afford to fight directly." Apollo gestured, and images appeared in the air between them—divine figures she recognized from mythology textbooks, their faces marked with indicators that suggested alliance or opposition. "Your mother has been the most consistent protector, though she operates from the shadows in ways that make my violations of cosmic law look trivial by comparison."

"Nyx has been helping?"

Apollo actually harrumphed. The moment made him appear almost human. "Nyx has been manipulating events to ensure Scion survival since the first mixed-blood children were born. Safe houses that appear when they're needed most, enemies who suffer convenient accidents, bureaucratic delays that prevent hunting teams from reaching their targets." Apollo's smile held genuine admiration. "She's turned violation of divine law into an art form."

The revelation that her mother had been actively protecting Scions, not just her but all of them, revised everything Alexis thought she understood about divine family relationships. Nyx wasn't an absent parent who had abandoned her daughter to mortal care. She was a cosmic force operating behind the scenes to ensure the survival of an entire category of beings.

"But even her influence has limits," Apollo continued. "Which is why direct intervention became necessary. Why I'm here, breaking laws that could cost me my immortality."

"To help us rescue Jamie?"

"To help you develop the abilities and knowledge necessary to stop Phthonos from implementing his final solution." Apollo stood, his divine radiance intensifying. "Because if he succeeds in accessing the Book of Fates, even Nyx won't be able to prevent the consequences."

Lily looked up from her workstation, where she'd been monitoring communications traffic from around the globe. "Speaking of consequences, we're seeing increased supernatural activity in major metropolitan areas. Government agencies are starting to notice patterns they can't explain."

"The masquerade is breaking down," Apollo confirmed. "Too many incidents, too much supernatural violence spilling into public view. We're approaching a tipping point where the existence of our kind becomes impossible to deny or cover up."

"What happens then?"

"Unknown territory. Humanity has never had to confront the reality of active divine intervention in their affairs. Some will adapt, some will panic, some will try to exploit the situation for personal gain." Apollo's expression grew grim. "But all of that becomes irrelevant if Phthonos succeeds in his plan."

Lily stood, moving to a map display that showed real-time tracking of supernatural incidents across North America. "Which brings us back to the immediate problem. Alexis needs to infiltrate his facility, gather intelligence on his defenses and timeline, and get out without triggering a response that could endanger Jamie."

"Agreed. But first, she needs to understand exactly what she'll be walking into." Apollo gestured, and the air filled with architectural diagrams and security assessments. "Phthonos has transformed a Manhattan office building into a fortress designed specifically to contain and control supernatural beings. Multiple layers of mystical wards, conventional security systems, and personnel trained to handle divine-level threats."

"Personnel like who?"

"Former military contractors with supernatural enhancement, Scions who've been turned against their own kind through psychological manipulation, and at least three divine beings who've allied themselves with his cause." The diagrams rotated, showing different levels of the building and their defensive measures. "The top floors have been converted into a mystical laboratory where he's attempting to interface Jamie's oracle abilities with the Book of Fates."

The clinical description of her best friend being used as a component in cosmic machinery made Alexis's power spike toward dangerous levels. Silver light began leaking from her skin, and she felt the careful control Lily had taught her threatening to shatter completely.

"Easy," Lily said, moving to her side. "Channel that anger into focus. You'll need every bit of control you can manage for this operation."

"How do I get in without being detected?"

"Through the building's mystical infrastructure," Apollo replied. "Every ward system has maintenance protocols, emergency overrides, and design flaws that can be exploited by someone with the right knowledge and abilities. I can provide you with access codes and structural weaknesses, but the execution will be entirely up to you."

"And if I'm caught?"

"Then you fight your way out and hope you can reach the ether before they overwhelm you. But capture isn't an option—Phthonos would use you as additional leverage against Jamie, possibly speeding up his timeline for the final phase." Apollo's expression grew deadly serious. "This is a reconnaissance mission only. Gather intelligence, confirm Jamie's location and condition, and extract without engagement."

"What about communication?"

Lily handed her a device that looked like a normal smartphone but radiated subtle mystical energy. "Encrypted quantum communication, shielded against supernatural detection. Check in every two hours, abort if you encounter anything beyond the expected security measures."

"And backup?"

"There is no backup," Apollo said bluntly. "If this operation goes wrong, you'll be on your own until you can reach extraction points we'll establish around the city. Hopefully, not something you'll need. The political cost of direct divine intervention in Manhattan would be... significant."

Alexis accepted the communication device and the weight of responsibility it represented. A solo infiltration mission into the heart of enemy territory, with the fate of reality itself potentially hanging in the balance.

"When do I leave?"

"Tonight," Lily replied. "The building's security protocols rotate on a seventy-two-hour cycle. Tonight represents the optimal window for minimal detection risk."

"Then I'd better finish my preparation." Alexis moved back toward the training area, but Apollo's voice stopped her.

"Alexis. There's something else you should know before you go."

"What?"

"If worse comes to worst, if Phthonos succeeds in beginning the rewriting process, there may be only one way to stop him." Apollo's expression carried the weight of cosmic knowledge she wasn't sure she wanted to possess. "The Book of Fates responds to will and intention backed by sufficient power. If Jamie can't prevent the process from starting, someone else might be able to override it."

"Someone else meaning me?"

"Meaning the daughter of Nyx who's learned to channel primordial power through mortal flesh. But the cost..." He paused, clearly reluctant to voice the implications. "The cost would be transformation into something that's no longer bound by the limitations of mortal existence. Something that could save reality itself but would never again be entirely human."

The warning echoed every caution she'd received about the price of cosmic power. But as Alexis thought about Keats trapped in a mystical laboratory, about the systematic elimination of everyone like her, about the rewriting of universal law to erase entire categories of beings from existence, the choice seemed obvious.

"I understand," she said.

"Do you?" Apollo's divine gaze seemed to see through flesh and bone to whatever lay beneath. "Because once you cross that threshold, there's no going back. You'd become something unprecedented—a force of nature walking in human form, wielding power that could remake the cosmos or destroy it completely."

"Then I'd better make sure I use it wisely."

Apollo studied her for a long moment, then nodded slowly. "Your mother would be proud. And probably terrified, but definitely proud."

As Alexis returned to her training, she felt the weight of destiny settling around her like armor. Tonight, she would infiltrate the stronghold of a god who wanted to erase her kind from existence. She would either gather reality-saving intelligence or die trying.

But either way, the war for the survival of Scions was about to enter its final phase.

And for the first time since this all began, she felt ready for whatever came next.

CHAPTER 17: THE MERIDIAN

The Manhattan skyline glittered beneath Alexis like a circuit board made of diamonds and steel, each window a potential sniper's nest, each shadow a place where enemies might wait. She crouched on the roof of a building a couple of blocks from her target, studying Phthonos's penthouse through high-powered night-vision binoculars while her enhanced senses cataloged every detail of the urban battlefield below.

The Meridian Tower thrust sixty stories into the night sky, its top floors converted into what intelligence reports described as a fortress designed specifically for containing supernatural beings. Mystical wards shimmered around the building's upper levels like heat distortion, visible only to those with divine sight. Security patrols moved in coordinated patterns across the lower floors, their movements too precise to be entirely human.

"This is Alpha," she whispered into her communication device. "Target building confirmed. Beginning approach."

Lily's voice crackled back through the encrypted channel. "Copy, Alpha. Remember—intelligence gathering only. Do not engage unless absolutely necessary."

"Understood." But even as she said it, Alexis felt power building beneath her skin like contained lightning, responding to the proximity of enemies who had taken everything that mattered to her.

She accessed the ether, stepping between dimensions to appear on the building's forty-second floor—high enough to avoid most security measures, low enough to stay below the heaviest mystical defenses. The transition was smoother than ever before, dimensional travel becoming as natural as walking through a doorway.

The office floor was empty at this hour, cubicles and conference rooms dark except for the ambient glow of limited lighting. But Alexis's enhanced senses detected the subtle wrongness that marked supernatural presence—a charged quality in the air that made her teeth ache and her vision sharpen to predatory focus.

She moved through the darkened office space with the fluid grace Lily had taught her, every step calculated to avoid detection by both technological and mystical sensors. The elevator bank stood at the center of the floor, surrounded by security cameras that tracked with mechanical precision.

Too easy. The thought whispered through her mind as she approached the maintenance access panel. Phthonos was a god, a being who had survived for millennia by outthinking his enemies. He wouldn't leave his stronghold vulnerable to infiltration by a teenage girl, no matter how divine her heritage.

Unless he wanted her to get inside.

The realization hit her like ice water, but she was already committed to the course of action. Keats was somewhere in this building—Apollo's intelligence had confirmed his presence through mystical scrying that couldn't be faked. Trap or not, she had to find him.

The maintenance shaft led upward through the building's infrastructure, past floors filled with humming servers and climate control equipment. She climbed in silence, using divine strength to move faster than human limitations would allow, until she reached the access point for the fifty-eighth floor.

Phthonos's personal domain.

The penthouse level stretched across the entire floor, an open space decorated with artifacts that radiated malevolent power. Ancient weapons hung on walls beside modern art, while pedestals displayed relics that hurt to look at directly. The air itself felt thick and oppressive, saturated with the psychic weight of accumulated envy and resentment.

"Welcome, sister."

The voice came from everywhere and nowhere, resonating through her bones with the authority of divine power. Phthonos materialized from shadow itself, appearing in the center of the room with the casual arrogance of someone operating on home territory.

He looked exactly as she remembered from Elizabeth's funeral—medium height, sharp features, expensive clothing that somehow made him appear larger than his physical dimensions. But here, in his own domain, the facade of mortality fell away completely. Power radiated from him like heat from a forge, and his eyes held the malevolent intelligence of something that had spent millennia nursing cosmic grudges.

"Did you really think it would be so easy?" he asked, moving closer with predatory grace. "That you could simply waltz into my sanctuary and steal away the key to universal revision?"

"Where is he?" Alexis kept her voice steady despite the fear building in her chest. "Where's Keats?"

"Safe. Protected. Being prepared for his role in the restoration of cosmic order." Phthonos smiled, and the expression was all sharp edges and hidden malice. "Though

I'm afraid visiting hours are quite limited."

"You're lying."

"Am I? Your friend is indeed here, suspended in an interface that allows his oracle abilities to commune with forces beyond mortal comprehension. Even now, he's learning to read the fundamental laws that govern existence itself." The smile widened. "Soon, he'll help me correct the aberration that your kind represents."

Power spiked beneath Alexis's skin, silver fire beginning to leak through her carefully maintained control. "He'll never help you. Jamie would die before he'd cooperate with anything you're planning."

"Death is always an option, of course. But I find psychological pressure far more effective than crude threats." Phthonos gestured, and the air shimmered with mystical energy that resolved into an image—Keats suspended in some kind of crystalline matrix, unconscious but clearly alive.

"As you can see, your friend is quite comfortable. And he'll remain so as long as his cooperation continues." The image shifted, showing other figures—Katy at the hospital, Aaron in his mountain facility, Lily in her cave network. All going about their daily routines, unaware they were being watched. "Of course, if he becomes... uncooperative... well, there are so many he cares about. So many potential pressure points."

The casual threat against innocent people ignited something primal in Alexis's chest. Rage—pure, cosmic fury that burned away rational thought and left only the need to destroy the source of that threat. The careful stealth protocols Lily had taught her evaporated like mist, replaced by power that made the air itself scream.

"You touch any of them and I'll—"

"You'll what?" Phthonos's voice carried amusement tinged with genuine interest.

"Destroy me? Remake reality according to your will? Become the very thing these mortals fear most about our kind?" He circled her like a predator evaluating prey. "That's what I'm counting on, sister. Your transformation into something that proves their fears are justified."

The words hit her like physical blows, laying bare the psychological trap he'd been weaving since their first encounter. Every escalation, every act of violence, every choice that moved her further from her human origins—all of it designed to transform her into evidence that Scions were too dangerous to exist.

"You killed our parents," she said, forcing her voice to remain steady while power built toward explosive release. "You murdered Charles in our living room."

"I eliminated obstacles to cosmic necessity. Charles Rain was protecting an aberration that threatened universal stability. Elizabeth Rain was..." He paused, tilting his head as if considering a complex equation. "Actually, Elizabeth's death was quite accidental. A miscalculation on the part of mortal agents who exceeded their instructions."

The casual admission hit her like a sledgehammer. Elizabeth—kind, caring Elizabeth who had raised her with love and patience—killed by incompetent subordinates carrying out Phthonos's orders. Not a calculated murder but a bureaucratic error in a campaign of cosmic genocide.

"You didn't even mean to kill her."

"Regrettable, certainly. But ultimately irrelevant to the larger purpose." Phthonos stopped circling, fixing her with eyes that held the malevolent intensity of black holes. "Which is the permanent elimination of every mixed-blood child who threatens the natural order of existence."

"We're not threats. We're people."

"You're chaos incarnate," Phthonos said, his voice carrying the weight of millennia. "I've watched civilizations rise and fall because one half-blood child couldn't control their inheritance. Atlantis. Lemuria. Entire peoples erased because we allowed divine power to flow through mortal vessels too weak to contain it. You call it genocide—I call it vaccination against cosmic plague."

"Then why not just kill us? Why this elaborate manipulation, this psychological warfare?"

"Because simply murdering Scions creates martyrs and generates sympathy among the younger gods. But if I can demonstrate that divine-mortal hybrids inevitably become monsters—if I can show the cosmic community that you transform into precisely the threats they fear—then elimination becomes not just acceptable but necessary."

The scope of his manipulation became clear with crystalline clarity. Every trap, every escalation, every choice that forced her to become more violent and less human— all of it designed to prove his thesis about Scion nature. She was both his target and his evidence, a specimen being shaped into the very thing he claimed she had always been.

"And if I refuse to play your game?"

"Then your friend dies, slowly and painfully, while you watch. Then everyone you've ever cared about suffers the same fate. Then I find another Oracle, another key to unlock the Book of Fates, and implement the Restoration Protocol despite your resistance." His smile turned genuinely warm, which somehow made it infinitely more terrifying. "But I don't think you'll refuse. You're too human for that kind of strategic thinking."

"You're wrong about one thing," Alexis said, power finally reaching critical mass beneath her skin. "I'm not going to become a monster to prove your point."

"No?"

"I'm going to become something much worse." She let the full weight of her divine heritage flood through her, silver fire exploding from her skin in waves that made reality itself groan under the strain. "I'm going to become the daughter of Nyx who doesn't give a damn about cosmic law when her family is threatened."

The penthouse erupted into chaos as her power met the mystical defenses built into the building's structure. Wards designed to contain supernatural beings shattered like glass, while security systems overloaded and died in showers of sparks. The very air began to writhe and twist as dimensional barriers grew thin under the pressure of primordial energy.

Phthonos weathered the initial assault with the practiced ease of someone who had faced cosmic-level threats before, his own power rising to meet hers in a clash that sent shockwaves through the building's foundation. But even as their forces met and grappled, Alexis felt something wrong—a presence behind her that radiated familiar supernatural signature.

She spun around just in time to see Harsh Dewan emerge from concealment near the elevator bank, assault rifle tracking toward her center mass with military precision. Aaron's half-brother moved with the fluid grace that marked divine heritage, but his eyes held the flat assessment of someone who had made peace with necessary violence.

"Hello, Alexis," he said, his voice carrying none of the warmth she remembered from her encounters with his brother in the Caucasus. "I'm afraid this conversation is over."

The betrayal hit her harder than any physical blow. Harsh was of course working for Phthonos.

"Aaron trusted you," she said, power redirecting toward this new threat while

Phthonos watched with obvious satisfaction.

"Aaron is naive. He believes family loyalty trumps cosmic necessity." Harsh's finger tightened on the trigger, but his aim remained steady and professional. "I believe in preventing the end of everything."

"By helping a god commit genocide?"

"By stopping an aberration from destroying the universe." The rifle's muzzle never wavered from her heart. "You have no idea what you really are, do you? What kind of cosmic disruption your existence represents?"

"Enlighten me."

"You're the daughter of Nyx—primordial goddess of night, one of the fundamental forces that shaped reality itself. Your very existence tears holes in the barriers between dimensions, creates instabilities that could unravel the fabric of space-time." His voice carried the conviction of someone stating mathematical facts. "Every time you access the ether, every time you manifest that silver fire, you weaken the cosmic infrastructure that keeps existence stable."

The accusation reframed everything she thought she understood about her abilities. Not gifts, but symptoms of cosmic disease. Not evolution, but corruption that threatened the survival of reality itself.

"That's impossible."

"Is it? How many dimensional barriers have you shattered in the past month? How many times have you stepped between worlds without understanding the consequences?" Harsh's expression grew troubled, suggesting this conversation was causing him genuine pain. "Aaron sees what he wants to see—family that needs protection. I see the truth—power that needs to be contained before it destroys everything."

"Then you're both fools."

Phthonos's voice cut through their confrontation with the authority of divine judgment. "She cannot be contained, only eliminated. Her power grows stronger every day, every use of her abilities creates more damage to cosmic stability. Soon, she'll reach a threshold where her mere existence becomes incompatible with universal law."

"Which is why the Restoration Protocol is necessary," Harsh agreed, though his voice carried reluctance that suggested the conclusion had come at significant personal cost. "Erase Scions from the timeline before they accumulate enough power to break everything."

"You're both insane." Alexis felt dimensional barriers growing thin around her as her emotional state destabilized her connection to normal reality. "People aren't cosmic disasters waiting to happen. We're just trying to survive in a world that wants us dead."

"Survival that comes at the cost of universal stability is not survival worth preserving." Harsh's rifle never wavered, but she caught the slight tension in his stance that suggested he was preparing to fire. "I'm sorry, Alexis. This isn't personal."

"It is to me."

She accessed the ether, stepping between dimensions to appear behind him before he could track her movement. But Harsh had been expecting the maneuver—his divine heritage included enhanced reflexes that let him spin and fire even as she materialized, the specialized rounds designed to disrupt supernatural healing tearing through her shoulder and side.

Pain blazed through her nervous system, but rage burned hotter. This was Charles's killer—the man who had been sent to murder her father in their living room, who had broken everything that made their house a home. Personal grievance met cosmic fury as she channeled the full weight of her inheritance into physical assault.

Harsh possessed superior training and equipment, but Alexis fought with the primal intensity of someone defending everything she had left to lose. She burned through the pain of the bullets and disarmed Harsh with excessive force. They crashed into physical combat, tearing through the penthouse's expensive furnishings, trading blows that would have killed normal humans, while Phthonos watched with the detached interest of someone evaluating experimental data.

Harsh managed to get his hands around her throat, divine strength beginning to crush her windpipe, but Alexis drove silver fire directly into his nervous system. The energy burned through his defenses like acid through paper, disrupting the divine enhancement that gave him superhuman resilience.

He released her with a scream that held both pain and genuine surprise, staggering backward toward the penthouse's floor-to-ceiling windows. Blood ran from his eyes and nose where the mystical backlash had ruptured blood vessels, and his movements had lost their supernatural coordination.

"You killed my father," Alexis said, advancing with power building around her like a storm front. "You broke into our home and murdered him in our living room."

"Orders," Harsh gasped, divine healing working to repair the damage she'd inflicted. "Nothing personal. Just orders."

"It was personal to me."

She hit him with everything she had—months of accumulated grief and rage and betrayal focused into a single assault that shattered his remaining defenses completely. The impact sent him crashing through the reinforced window in an explosion of glass and twisted metal, his body tumbling toward the street sixty stories below.

But the force of her own attack carried her forward, momentum and shattered window frame providing no purchase to stop her fall. For a moment that stretched into eternity, she found herself falling beside her father's killer, Manhattan's lights blurring past them in streaks of color and motion.

Harsh's eyes met hers during that shared descent, and she saw something that might have been regret or relief before he spoke his final words.

"Tell Aaron... I'm sorry."

Then she accessed the ether, stepping between dimensions while Harsh continued his fall toward the unforgiving pavement below. It may have been her imagination but she could have sworn, just before she slipped into the ether, that she heard the distinct sound of horse's hooves. She emerged in the space between spaces, that familiar grayness that had become her sanctuary, and felt the moment when divine enhancement met immutable physics sixty stories down.

Harsh Dewan—son of Ares, former Army Ranger, professional killer who specialized in hunting Scions—was dead. She had killed him with deliberate intent, crossing a line that could never be uncrossed.

The realization should have triggered guilt, horror, some kind of emotional response to the magnitude of what she'd done. Instead, she felt only cold satisfaction and the terrible clarity that came from serving justice with her own hands.

Charles was avenged. But Keats was still lost, and she was no closer to finding him than before.

Somewhere, Phthonos's laughter echoed through dimensional barriers with the sound of cosmic malice given voice. He had gotten exactly what he wanted—proof that Scions inevitably became the monsters everyone feared.

Now she had to find another way to save her best friend before that transformation became complete.

The war for her soul was far from over.

But the first major battle had just been lost.

CHAPTER 18: A DEAL IS MADE

The ether embraced Alexis like a mother's arms, its gray expanse offering sanctuary from the violence and betrayal that had shattered her understanding of right and wrong. She floated in the space between dimensions, letting the cosmic silence wash away the sound of Harsh's final words and the memory of his body meeting Manhattan pavement sixty stories below.

Tell Aaron... I'm sorry.

The words echoed through her consciousness with the weight of genuine regret, complicating what should have been a moment of pure satisfaction. She had killed her father's murderer, served justice with her own hands, crossed the line from defender to executioner. But instead of closure, she felt only the hollow certainty that violence bred more violence, that every choice moved her further from the person she'd been and closer to something she didn't recognize.

The ether responded to her emotional state, its neutral grayness shifting toward darker hues that reflected her inner turmoil. Here, in the space between realities, she existed as pure consciousness unbound by physical limitations or moral constraints. The daughter of Nyx in her element, drawing strength from darkness itself.

But sanctuary wouldn't save Keats. And sitting in dimensional limbo wouldn't provide answers about how to find him now that Phthonos's trap had closed without revealing his true location.

Alexis focused her will, shaping the ether around her into something more useful than an emotional refuge. If this space responded to intention, if it could serve as more than just a means of travel, then perhaps she could use it for strategic planning. The vast library of human knowledge she could access might be more accessible here, where the boundaries between mind and reality grew thin.

The gray expanse transformed, cosmic darkness giving way to towering shelves that stretched beyond visual range. Books, scrolls, digital files, and information stored in formats that had no names—all of it organized according to some ineffable system that existed outside normal space-time. Her divine heritage had given her access to humanity's accumulated knowledge, but here she could navigate that information with supernatural efficiency.

She pulled relevant data streams toward her consciousness, searching for leads that conventional intelligence gathering had missed. Financial records showing shell companies that funded supernatural research. Communication intercepts between government agencies dealing with unexplained incidents. Academic papers on subjects that officially didn't exist.

And there—a name buried in classified documents that made her divine senses tingle with recognition.

Emerson Greer.

The information cascaded through her awareness like water through a broken dam. CEO of Greer Entertainment, one of Hollywood's most powerful talent agencies. Publicly known for representing A-list actors and directing blockbuster films. Privately connected to a network that bought and sold supernatural artifacts on the black market.

More significantly, he was listed in Aaron's intelligence files as a potential broker of information about Scion locations. Someone who traded in supernatural secrets for the right price.

The trail led to Los Angeles, to the entertainment industry that thrived on illusion and the careful management of public perception. If Greer really did have connections to the supernatural underground, he might know where Phthonos had taken Keats. And if he was willing to deal in information, she had currency that might interest him.

Alexis shaped her will toward a new destination, stepping through dimensional barriers to emerge in an alley behind a Sunset Boulevard nightclub. The transition from ether to normal reality hit her like a physical shock—the sudden weight of flesh and bone, the assault of sensory input that included car exhaust and cigarette smoke and the bass line from whatever band was playing inside.

Los Angeles spread around her like a neon fever dream, all palm trees and traffic lights and beautiful people pursuing impossible dreams. The entertainment capital of the world, where reality was negotiable and perception shaped truth more than facts. The perfect place for someone trafficking in supernatural secrets to hide in plain sight.

But before she could approach Greer, she needed information about his operation. And according to Aaron's files, that meant talking to someone who moved in the same circles but operated with different goals.

Rayleigh Towne held court at an exclusive rooftop club in West Hollywood, surrounded by the kind of beautiful people who gravitated toward power like moths toward flame. The daughter of Aphrodite commanded attention without effort, her presence drawing every gaze in the room despite the fierce competition from actors and models who made their living on physical perfection.

She was tall—nearly six feet—with honey-blonde hair that moved in slow waves and eyes the color of summer storms. Her dress cost more than most people made in a month, but she wore it with the casual confidence of someone to whom material possessions were just tools for achieving larger goals.

More dangerously, she radiated an aura of irresistible attraction that made everyone in her vicinity want to please her, to gain her approval, to offer whatever she might desire. Divine heritage expressing itself through supernatural charisma that could bend minds and reshape wills.

"Alexis Rain," Rayleigh said without turning around, her voice carrying the kind of honey-sweet poison that made dangerous offers sound reasonable. "Daughter of Nyx, killer of gods' children, seeker of information that doesn't want to be found. You've caused quite a stir in certain circles."

"Word travels fast."

"Everything travels fast in this city. Information, gossip, reputation—it all moves at the speed of light and usually gets distorted in the process." Rayleigh finally turned to face her, and Alexis felt the full weight of supernatural seduction pressing against her consciousness. "Though in your case, the reality seems more impressive than the rumors."

The psychic pressure intensified, attempting to bypass rational thought and appeal directly to emotional and physical responses. Alexis felt her pulse quicken and her breathing deepen as Aphrodite's influence worked to make her more receptive to suggestion, more willing to cooperate with whatever Rayleigh wanted. This was a test. And, Rayleigh leaned into it with fervor. Her cosmic -born abilities to light the fire of passion in others. Her ability to impart the seductiveness of attraction on unsuspecting targets. She laid it on thick, pushing into Alexis' emotions and desires and triggering a flood of dopamine into Alexis' system. The power was undeniable. The blanket of desire warming her through to the bone.

But the daughter of Nyx had advantages that most lacked. She was, after all, the daughter of the most seductive creature in existence. Power flowed through her veins, and night itself offered protection against influence that relied on light and beauty and conventional attraction. She reached for the darkness that lived in her bones, using primordial authority to shield her mind from divine manipulation. She pulled in all that Rayleigh was throwing at her and redirected it back to its owner. The tidal wave fell over the actress and she staggered and sat down in a slow but desperate move to hide her failure.

"Interesting," Rayleigh murmured, her expression shifting from confident control to genuine curiosity. She shook off her own effects and stared at Alexis for a long moment. "Most people can't resist that level of influence. Either you're much stronger than I expected, or you're not as human as you appear."

"Little of both, probably." Alexis moved closer, noting how the crowd around them unconsciously shifted to give her space. Her divine signature was affecting normal humans the same way Rayleigh's affected her—marking her as something that operated outside conventional social rules. "I need information."

"Information about what?"

"Emerson Greer. His business relationships, his supernatural connections, how to approach him without ending up dead or disappeared." She studied Rayleigh's reaction, looking for tells that might indicate deception or hidden agendas. "Aaron Richardson's files suggest you've had dealings with him before."

"Aaron." Rayleigh's laugh held notes of genuine amusement. "Such a serious boy, always so worried about protecting our kind from forces beyond our control. He thinks building networks and gathering intelligence will somehow make us safe from people who want us extinct."

"You disagree?"

"I think survival requires adaptation. Evolution. Becoming something that can't be threatened by mortals or their divine allies." Rayleigh gestured toward the crowd of beautiful people who hung on her every word despite not being able to hear the conversation. "These humans worship at the altar of celebrity and superficial perfection. They'll literally kill themselves trying to achieve the kind of beauty and charisma I was born with. Why should I hide what I am when I can use it to build an empire?"

"And Greer? How does he fit into your empire-building?"

"Emerson trades in supernatural artifacts, as I'm sure you already know—objects of power that can enhance abilities or provide protection from mystical threats. Very useful for those of us who prefer to operate in the open rather than hiding in mountain caves." Rayleigh's storm-colored eyes fixed on Alexis with laser intensity. "But his services don't come cheap. He requires payment in favors, secrets, or objects of equivalent value."

"What kind of favors?"

"The kind that usually involve stealing things from people who don't want to give them up. Greer has expensive tastes and powerful enemies, which means he needs equally powerful allies to stay alive." Rayleigh stood and moved a little closer, her supernatural aura intensifying as she tried to gauge Alexis's reaction. "Tell me, daughter of night—how far are you willing to go to save your Oracle friend?"

The question carried implications that made Alexis's blood run cold. Not just risk, but moral compromise. Not just danger, but the kind of choices that changed people permanently.

"As far as necessary."

"Even if it means stealing from the gods themselves?"

The words hung in the air between them like a loaded weapon, carrying the weight of cosmic transgression and consequences that could reshape the supernatural world. But before Alexis could respond, a new voice cut through their conversation with the authority of someone accustomed to holding everyone's attention.

"Ms. Rain. Ms. Towne. How delightful to see you both here."

Emerson Greer appeared beside their table with the silent grace of someone who had learned to move through crowds with ease. He was older than she'd expected—maybe thirty—with silver-blonde hair and the kind of tan that came from years of California sunshine. His suit probably cost more than some people's cars, but he moved with the casual confidence of someone who had never worried about money.

More significantly, he radiated the same supernatural pressure that marked divine heritage. Not as overwhelming as Rayleigh's seductive influence or as alien as Phthonos's cosmic malice, but unmistakably inhuman nonetheless.

"Mr. Greer," Rayleigh said, her tone shifting to match the formality he'd introduced. "I wasn't expecting to see you tonight."

"Business brings me to the most unexpected places. And speaking of business—" His attention shifted to Alexis with the focused intensity of a predator who had found interesting prey. "I understand you're looking for information about someone who's recently acquired a very valuable asset."

"You know about Keats?"

"I know about many things. Oracle children, books that contain the fundamental laws of reality, gods who believe they can rewrite existence according to their personal preferences." Greer settled into the booth across from them, his presence somehow making the loud nightclub feel intimate and private. "I also know that finding such information requires payment in kind."

"What kind of payment?" Alexis observed the flash of something in Greer's face and knew she was about to be bamboozled. This man seemed as if he'd made it his life's work to manipulate deals and get what he wanted. The problem was that Alexis hated to be manipulated. With a passion.

"There's an auction happening tomorrow night. Very exclusive, very illegal, very dangerous. The kind of gathering where divine artifacts change hands for prices that would bankrupt small nations." His smile was sharp and professional. "One particular item being offered is of significant interest to me—Hermes' caduceus, stolen from Mount Olympus itself, what, three centuries ago."

Alexis felt the universe tilt sideways. "You want me to steal from the gods."

"I want you to acquire an artifact that rightfully belongs to someone who will use it more responsibly than its current owners. The distinction is important for legal and moral purposes." Greer's expression grew serious. "In exchange, I'll provide you with real-time intelligence about Phthonos's current location and operational security. Everything you need to mount a successful rescue operation."

"And if I refuse?"

"Then your Oracle friend remains lost, the Book of Fates gets used to erase every Scion from existence, including us…and, reality gets rewritten according to the whims of a god who believes diversity is a cosmic mistake." He shrugged eloquently. "Your choice, of course. But choose quickly—the auction happens in thirty-six hours, and preparation takes time."

Rayleigh leaned forward, her supernatural aura pulsing with interest. "What aren't you telling us about this caduceus? Divine artifacts don't just sit around in illegal auctions without serious protection."

"The item in question is currently owned by someone with extensive resources and very little patience for thieves. Security will include both technological and mystical defenses, plus personnel trained specifically to handle supernatural threats." Greer's smile turned predatory. "But then, Ms. Rain, you've already demonstrated considerable skill at infiltrating heavily defended facilities."

"You heard about the penthouse."

"I hear about everything that affects the supernatural community's delicate balance. Your confrontation with Phthonos and subsequent elimination of Harsh Dewan has created ripples that are being felt across multiple power structures." His expression grew troubled. "Some of those ripples are approaching tsunami levels."

"Meaning?"

"Meaning your actions have consequences beyond personal vengeance. The death of Ares' son at the hands of Nyx's daughter has attracted attention from cosmic forces that prefer to avoid direct involvement in mortal affairs." Greer pulled out a tablet and showed her surveillance footage that made her blood freeze. "Divine politics are heating up, and you're at the center of the storm." He nodded nonchalantly at the huge TV hanging above the bar to their left.

The screen showed scenes from around the world—unexplained phenomena, natural disasters, government officials receiving visits from people who didn't appear in any databases. The masquerade that kept supernatural reality hidden from public awareness was breaking down, and her escalating conflict with Phthonos was accelerating the collapse.

"Zeus himself has called for a divine assembly to address the 'Scion situation,'" Greer continued. "The outcome of that meeting will determine whether our kind gets protection, regulation, or systematic elimination. Which means the clock isn't just ticking on your friend's rescue—it's ticking on the survival of every mixed-blood child in existence."

The weight of cosmic responsibility settled on Alexis's shoulders like lead armor. Not just Keats's life, but the future of everyone like her hanging in the balance. Every choice she made, every action she took, rippling outward to affect forces and conflicts she barely understood.

"The caduceus," she said finally. "What makes it so important to you?"

"Let's just say that some divine artifacts are useful for more than their traditional purposes." His smile turned genuinely warm, which somehow made it infinitely more terrifying. "Very useful when dealing with immortals."

The implication hung in the air like poison gas. Greer didn't just want the caduceus for its mystical properties—he wanted it as a weapon against divine beings. Which raised the question of which god he intended to kill, and whether helping him acquire such a weapon made her complicit in cosmic assassination.

"Twenty-four hours," she said. "I get you the caduceus, you give me Phthonos's location."

"Agreed. But there's one more condition." Greer extended his hand, and she felt power building around them both as mystical forces prepared to bind their agreement. "This deal is sealed by divine oath. Break your word, and cosmic law will extract payment in ways that make death seem merciful."

Alexis looked at his outstretched hand, knowing that accepting would bind her to a course of action with consequences she couldn't predict. But Keats was running out of time, and every hour of delay brought him closer to whatever role Phthonos intended him to play in the Restoration Protocol.

She took Greer's hand, feeling the surge of mystical energy that made their agreement binding on levels that transcended normal contracts. Power flowed between them, sealing the deal with authority that even gods would be forced to respect.

"Excellent," Greer said, releasing her hand with obvious satisfaction. "Here's the auction details," he said, handing her a small card with an address and a few other details. "And Ms. Rain? Try not to die before you complete our transaction. Divine oaths can be very unforgiving about unfulfilled obligations."

As he disappeared into the crowd with the same silent grace he'd used to approach, Alexis felt the weight of mystical compulsion settling around her like invisible chains. She was bound now, committed to a course of action that would require her to steal from beings who could crush her without effort.

But if it saved Keats and stopped the Restoration Protocol, it would be worth any price.

Even if that price was her soul.

CHAPTER 19: DIVINE THEFT

Alexis walked in silent thought down the beach, taking in the houses, searching for the specific one that she would infiltrate in order to steal a dangerous, cosmic artifact. She had to wonder if she had already gone crazy. She paused, turned to walk onto the pier as she went over everything from timing to the specific location of where she would need to step from the ether. Oh, and also how to try not to die.

The old fisherman sat there on the Malibu pier like he'd been carved from driftwood by salt spray, his weathered hands working a fishing line that disappeared into the Pacific's gray depths. Dawn was breaking over the California coast in streaks of gold and crimson, but he seemed oblivious to the beauty around him, focused entirely on whatever might be swimming in the waters below.

Alexis almost walked past him. She'd needed to think, to prepare mentally for the supernatural auction that would determine whether she could save Keats or doom herself trying. The mystical oath binding her to Greer's deal weighed on her consciousness like an invisible yoke, and she needed solitude to process the magnitude of what she was about to attempt.

But something about the fisherman made her pause. He was too still, too perfectly positioned, too precisely what someone would expect to find on a California pier at sunrise. Like a movie set designer's idea of authentic local color.

"Beautiful morning," he said without looking up from his line.

"If you like that sort of thing." She moved closer, noting details that didn't fit the image he was projecting. His clothes were worn but expensive, his posture suggested military training despite his apparent age, and his hands showed calluses that came from weapons work rather than fishing.

"Fish are biting well today. Caught three already. But I threw them back." He finally looked at her, and she felt the breath catch in her throat. His eyes held depths that spoke of knowledge accumulated over millennia, authority that could reshape reality with a thought. "Sometimes the best catches are the ones you don't keep."

Power radiated from him like heat from a forge, carefully contained but unmistakably divine. He was obviously powerful enough to hide his essence from until he was ready to reveal it. This certainly wasn't some random mortal enjoying a peaceful morning on the water. This was someone operating on a cosmic scale, wearing humanity like an ill-fitting disguise.

"Zeus," she said quietly.

"Just a fisherman enjoying the sunrise." His smile carried amusement tinged with something that might have been approval. "Though I suppose names have power, and power draws attention from those who monitor such things."

"Are you here to stop me?"

"Stop you from what? Enjoying a peaceful walk on the beach? Contemplating the eternal dance between sea and sky?" He reeled in his line, revealing a hook that held no bait. "I'm just an old man who enjoys the simple pleasures of mortal existence."

But his presence here, now, couldn't be coincidence. Zeus—king of the Olympian gods, ruler of divine politics, ultimate authority over cosmic law—didn't spend casual mornings fishing on California beaches. He was here for a reason, and that reason was probably connected to her mission.

"The auction," she said.

"Ah. Yes. I've heard whispers about such gatherings. Terrible things, really. Divine artifacts treated like commodities, sacred objects bought and sold by people who don't understand their significance. And, certainly, cannot understand how best to use them." He cast his line again, the motion fluid and practiced. "Of course, some artifacts are safer in private collections than in their original locations."

"Safer how?"

"Oh, I don't know. Let's consider… how about we consider Hermes' caduceus. Powerful artifact, capable of facilitating communication between realms, healing grievous wounds, even separating souls from bodies under the right circumstances." His tone remained conversational, but she caught the underlying current of warning. "In the wrong hands, it could cause considerable damage to cosmic stability."

"And in the right hands?"

"It might prevent an even greater catastrophe." He turned to face her fully, his casual fisherman disguise falling away to reveal the full weight of divine authority. "The question, young daughter of Nyx, is whether you can tell the difference between the right hands and the wrong ones."

The statement hung in the air between them like a challenge, loaded with implications about moral choices and cosmic consequences. Zeus knew about her deal with Greer, knew about the theft she was planning, and was apparently choosing not to prevent it.

"Why are you really here?"

"To observe. To evaluate. To determine whether the precedent you're setting serves the greater good or threatens the foundations of ordered existence." His expression grew serious. "Your actions have attracted attention from forces that prefer to avoid direct involvement in mortal affairs. Decisions are being made about the future of Scions, and those decisions will be influenced by what you do in the next twenty-four hours."

"No pressure, then."

"None at all." His smile returned, transforming his features from cosmic authority to benevolent grandfather. "Just a reminder that some fish are worth catching, some are better thrown back, and some will bite the hook no matter what bait you use."

Before she could ask what that meant, he was gone—not vanished in a display of divine power, but simply absent, as if he'd never been there at all. Only the lingering scent of ozone and the certainty that she'd just been evaluated by the king of gods himself remained.

The auction house squatted in downtown Los Angeles like a cancer disguised as urban renewal. From the outside, it looked like any other converted warehouse—concrete walls, industrial lighting, security cameras that tracked movement with mechanical precision. But Alexis's enhanced senses detected the wrongness that marked supernatural presence, a charged quality in the air that made her teeth ache.

She approached through the service entrance, using credentials Greer had provided along with warnings about the clientele she'd encounter inside. Buyers and sellers who traded in objects of power, information brokers who dealt in secrets that could topple governments, collectors who valued rarity over morality.

The kind of people who wouldn't hesitate to kill anyone who threatened their carefully maintained anonymity.

The outer security checkpoint was staffed by guards who moved with the fluid precision of enhanced reflexes, their eyes tracking her approach with predatory assessment. She submitted to the scanning procedures—electronic, mystical, and psychological—while projecting the aura of someone who belonged in this environment.

Rich. Dangerous. Completely indifferent to conventional morality.

"First time?" the guard asked, studying readouts that apparently satisfied whatever criteria they were monitoring.

"Business brings me to the most unexpected places."

"Doesn't it always." He handed her a tablet displaying the evening's catalog—artifacts, information, and services arranged according to some system that prioritized value over legality. "Bidding starts in thirty minutes. Payment is expected immediately following successful acquisition."

She moved deeper into the warehouse, noting escape routes and security measures while studying the other attendees. Most looked like wealthy eccentrics with more money than sense, but her divine heritage let her sense the supernatural signatures that revealed their true nature.

Scions hiding their abilities behind expensive clothes and practiced arrogance. Minor gods operating through mortal intermediaries. Government agents whose presence suggested official interest in monitoring supernatural commerce.

And scattered throughout the crowd, individuals who radiated the kind of malevolent power that made normal humans unconsciously step aside.

The auction floor stretched across the warehouse's central space, with items displayed on pedestals that hummed with containment fields. Divine artifacts that hurt to look at directly sat beside technological devices that shouldn't have existed for another decade, at least. Information was sold alongside objects, secrets packaged as commodities for those with deep enough pockets.

She found the caduceus near the center of the display area, mounted on a pedestal that bristled with more security measures than the others. Hermes' staff gleamed with inner light that seemed to pulse in rhythm with her heartbeat, its twin serpents writhing with barely contained energy.

"Beautiful, isn't it?"

The voice belonged to a woman who looked like she'd stepped out of a fashion magazine—tall, elegant, wearing a dress that likely cost more than Alexis wanted to think about. But underneath the surface beauty, Alexis sensed something vast and alien, intelligence that operated on scales that made human concerns seem trivial.

"It's certainly impressive," she replied carefully.

"Hermes was always so proud of that particular creation. The perfect fusion of divine power and artistic expression, capable of bridging gaps between realms that were never meant to be crossed." The woman moved closer, her presence making the air itself seem to vibrate with potential energy. "Of course, its current owners don't appreciate its full significance."

"And who might that be?"

"Private collectors who value rarity over responsibility. The kind of people who display priceless artifacts like hunting trophies, never understanding the consequences of removing such objects from their proper context." Her smile carried implications that made Alexis's blood run cold. "But perhaps tonight will see it returned to more appropriate custody."

Before Alexis could respond, the auction began. Items moved across the block with ruthless efficiency—artifacts that could level cities sold to buyers who hid behind numbered paddles and electronic transfers. Information about Scion locations, government supernatural programs, and divine political movements changed hands for prices that would have funded small wars.

The caduceus came up for bidding two hours into the proceedings. Starting price: fifty million dollars. The number climbed steadily as paddles rose and fell around the warehouse, wealthy collectors competing for the privilege of owning one of mythology's most famous artifacts.

Alexis waited until the bidding reached its peak before making her move. Instead of raising a paddle, she accessed the ether, stepping between dimensions to appear on the auction floor beside the caduceus's pedestal. Alarms began shrieking as security systems registered the breach, but she was already grabbing the staff and preparing to retreat into dimensional transit.

The moment her fingers closed around the caduceus, power blazed through her nervous system like liquid lightning. Not painful, but overwhelming—information and energy flowing through channels she hadn't known existed. The staff was alive, aware, evaluating her worthiness to wield power that could reshape reality itself.

Interesting, a voice whispered in her mind. *Very interesting indeed.*

Security forces converged on her position with inhuman speed, but she was already stepping back into the ether, the stolen artifact clutched against her chest. The transition should have been smooth, natural, effortless.

Instead, she found herself trapped between dimensions, suspended in grayness that felt different from the welcoming darkness she'd come to associate with the space between worlds. This wasn't sanctuary—it was a cosmic waiting room where forces beyond mortal comprehension could conduct business without interference.

"Alexis Rain, daughter of Nyx, thief of divine artifacts."

The voice came from everywhere and nowhere, carrying authority that made Zeus's presence seem trivial by comparison. Three figures materialized from the ether's gray expanse, their forms shifting between human appearance and something far more fundamental.

The Fates. The Moirai. The three sisters who controlled destiny itself.

Clotho, who spun the threads of life, appeared as a young woman whose hands moved in constant, minute gestures that suggested she was weaving reality from raw possibility. Lachesis, who measured those threads, looked middle-aged and carried instruments that gleamed with cosmic significance. Atropos, who cut the threads when their time was done, seemed ancient beyond measure, her shears capable of severing connections that held the universe together.

"You have taken something that does not belong to you," Clotho said, her voice carrying the weight of infinite potential. "An artifact whose removal from proper custody creates... complications."

"Complications in what?"

"The pattern we have been weaving for centuries. Plans that require precise timing, careful coordination, exact placement of key individuals at critical moments." Lachesis gestured, and images appeared in the ether around them—scenes from past and future that showed Alexis's actions rippling outward through time itself. "Your theft has introduced variables that threaten outcomes we have spent considerable effort to arrange."

"Unless," Atropos added, her ancient voice carrying finality that could end worlds, "you prove capable of serving our purposes as well as your own."

The statement hung in the cosmic silence like a loaded weapon. The Fates—beings who wrote destiny itself—were offering her some kind of deal. But their purposes operated on scales that made her personal concerns seem insignificant.

"What do you want?"

"Cooperation. Understanding. Acceptance that some patterns serve purposes greater than individual desire." Clotho's hands continued their weaving motions, threads of possibility twisting into configurations that hurt to perceive directly. "The Restoration Protocol represents a knot in the cosmic web, a disruption that could unravel more than just Scion existence."

"You're saying Phthonos's plan threatens more than just people like me?"

"We are saying that reality itself has certain... structural requirements. Remove too many threads from the pattern, and the entire weaving begins to collapse." Lachesis showed her images that made her mind reel—cosmic forces in balance, divine politics maintaining stability through careful tension, the delicate ecosystem of existence depending on diversity rather than purity.

"Which is why we offer this." Atropos extended something that looked like a pendant carved from crystallized starlight. "Knowledge that will serve you in the trials ahead, guidance that will help you choose correctly when the final moment arrives."

"What kind of knowledge?"

"The location of the true Book of Fates. The understanding you will need to read it correctly. The wisdom to use its power without destroying everything you seek to protect." The ancient sister's expression grew grave. "But also the burden of knowing that some victories require sacrifices you are not prepared to make."

Alexis stared at the pendant, understanding that accepting it would bind her to purposes she didn't fully comprehend. But Keats was running out of time, and the Restoration Protocol was moving toward implementation whether she understood the cosmic implications or not.

She took the pendant, feeling knowledge flood through her consciousness like ice water through her veins. Images, concepts, understanding that existed on levels her mortal mind could barely process. The true nature of reality, the fundamental forces that shaped existence, the terrible choice that would define the future of everything.

"Use it wisely," Clotho said as the ether began to release her back to normal reality. "The pattern requires both change and stability, growth and preservation. Your role is to ensure that balance is maintained."

"And if I fail?"

"Then everything ends," Atropos replied with the finality of absolute truth. "Not just Scions, not just gods, but existence itself. The pattern unravels, and what remains is less than nothing."

The grayness dissolved around her, depositing her in a Malibu parking garage with the caduceus still clutched in her hands and cosmic knowledge burning through her skull like acid. She staggered against a concrete pillar, overwhelmed by the weight of what she'd learned and the magnitude of the choice she would soon face.

Her phone buzzed with an incoming message from Greer: Acquisition confirmed. Meet at the designated location to complete our transaction.

She made her way to the beachfront restaurant where Greer waited in a private dining room, his expression mixing satisfaction with barely concealed anticipation. The caduceus lay on the table between them, its divine radiance making the expensive furnishings seem tawdry by comparison.

"Excellent work," he said, not reaching for the staff despite obvious desire to claim it. "Though I understand you encountered some... complications during the extraction process."

"Nothing I couldn't handle."

"The Fates rarely involve themselves in mortal affairs so directly. Their intervention suggests your actions have consequences beyond what either of us anticipated." His expression grew troubled. "But no matter. A deal is a deal, and divine oaths are binding regardless of circumstances."

He produced a tablet displaying real-time surveillance footage that made her breath catch in her throat. A compound in rural Ontario, heavily fortified and warded against supernatural detection. But the mystical signatures were unmistakable—the same energy pattern she'd felt around Phthonos in the Manhattan penthouse.

"Industrial complex on the shore of Lake Huron. Purchased through shell companies three months ago and converted into what intelligence reports describe as a research facility." Greer highlighted specific buildings and defensive positions. "Your Oracle friend is being held in the central laboratory, along with the artifact your brother intends to use for universal revision."

"The Book of Fates."

"Hidden there for safekeeping while he prepares the final phase of his plan. Security includes both technological and mystical defenses, plus personnel trained specifically to handle divine-level threats." He looked up from the tablet with genuine concern. "This won't be another simple infiltration mission. This will be war."

"I've been preparing for war since the day he killed my father."

"Have you?" Greer finally reached for the caduceus, his fingers closing around its shaft with reverent care. "Because there's something you should know about our transaction. Something I perhaps should have mentioned earlier."

"Which is?"

"This artifact isn't just useful for facilitating communication between realms. In the right hands, with the proper knowledge, it can be used to kill someone who's technically immortal." His smile turned sharp and predatory. "Someone like a god who's forgotten that divine status doesn't make them untouchable."

The implication hit her like ice water. She hadn't just stolen an artifact for Greer—she'd provided him with a weapon capable of divine assassination. Whatever his ultimate plans, they involved killing a god, and she'd just made it possible.

"Who?" she asked, though part of her already knew the answer.

"Someone who's done terrible things in the name of *cosmic law*." Greer stood, the caduceus disappearing into whatever mystical storage he used for supernatural contraband. "Don't look so troubled, Ms. Rain. Gods have been killing each other since the dawn of creation. I'm simply... updating the methodology."

As he left her alone with the intelligence about Phthonos's compound and the terrible knowledge that she'd enabled cosmic assassination, Alexis felt the weight of destiny settling around her like a weighted blanket. The Fates had warned her about choices and consequences, about patterns that served purposes greater than individual desire.

Now she understood why they'd been concerned.

She'd just provided someone with the means to kill a god, and she had no idea which divine being was about to die—or what their death might unleash on a universe that was already teetering on the edge of chaos.

But Keats was running out of time, and the Restoration Protocol was moving toward implementation regardless of her moral qualms about cosmic assassination.

The war for the future of their existence was about to begin in earnest.

And, now, she was no longer certain which side she was fighting for.

CHAPTER 20: PREPARATION FOR WAR

The command center carved into the Georgian mountains felt smaller when Alexis stepped out of the ether, as if the weight of cosmic knowledge and divine assassination had compressed the familiar space into something claustrophobic. Aaron looked up from his surveillance monitors, his expression shifting from relief to wariness as he processed the changes in her posture and bearing. Apparently, he'd showed up after she'd gone.

"You look like hell," he said, moving away from his workstation to study her more closely. "And you feel different. More dangerous."

"Recent developments have been... educational." She settled into one of the tactical chairs, noting how the mystical pendant the Fates had given her seemed to pulse in rhythm with her heartbeat. "I have intelligence on Phthonos's location. Current, verified, actionable intelligence."

"That's good news. What's the bad news?"

The question hung in the air between them, loaded with the certainty that good intelligence always came at a price. Alexis thought about Harsh's final words, about the sound of hooves in the air, about the sound his body had made hitting Manhattan pavement, about the terrible satisfaction she'd felt watching her father's killer die.

"Your brother's dead."

Aaron went very still, his breathing becoming shallow and controlled in the way that suggested emotional shock carefully contained. He'd been preparing for this possibility since learning about Harsh's allegiance to Phthonos, but knowing something intellectually was different from facing its reality.

"How?" he asked finally.

"We fought. He lost." She met his gaze steadily, refusing to soften the truth with euphemisms or justifications. "It was my choice, Aaron. I could have found another way, but I chose to kill him instead."

"Why?"

"Because he murdered my father. Because he was working for the god who wants to erase every Scion from existence. Because in that moment, justice mattered more than mercy." She leaned forward, power beginning to stir beneath her skin. "And because he was about to kill me, and I decided I had more important things to do than die in a Manhattan penthouse."

Aaron processed this information with the methodical precision of someone who had learned to compartmentalize emotional trauma. His hands moved in small, unconscious gestures that might have been prayer or simply the need to keep them occupied while his mind worked through implications.

"Did he say anything? At the end?"

"He asked me to tell you he was sorry."

The words hit their target with surgical precision. Aaron's carefully maintained composure cracked, revealing grief that went beyond simple loss. Harsh hadn't just been his half-brother—he'd been a partner, a friend, someone who had shared the burden of divine heritage in a world that wanted people like them dead.

"Sorry for what? Choosing the wrong side? Getting himself killed? Twenty years of brotherhood thrown away for cosmic ideology?" Aaron's voice carried bitterness that spoke of old arguments and fundamental disagreements. "Or sorry for making me watch while he turned into everything we swore we'd never become?"

"I don't know. He just said to tell you he was sorry."

"Well, he was. Sorry and stupid and so convinced he was saving the universe that he couldn't see he was helping to destroy it." Aaron stood abruptly, moving to the weapons locker with movements that were too controlled, too precise. "But that doesn't change the tactical situation. We still need to stop Phthonos, and we still need to rescue your Oracle friend."

"Aaron—"

"Don't." He pulled out an assault rifle and began checking its action with mechanical efficiency. "I knew this day would come. I've been preparing for it since Harsh made his choice to serve the enemy. The only surprise is that you're the one who finally put him down."

The clinical tone worried her more than open grief would have. Aaron was compartmentalizing, shoving emotional responses aside to focus on immediate tactical concerns. It was a survival mechanism she understood—she'd done the same thing after Charles's murder. But it was also dangerous, the kind of psychological strategy that worked short-term but left permanent damage.

"We need to talk about the intelligence I gathered," she said, changing the subject to something more immediately actionable. "Phthonos is operating out of an industrial complex in rural Ontario. Heavy security, mystical wards, personnel trained specifically to handle supernatural threats."

"What kind of personnel?"

"Unknown. But the facility is large enough to house significant defensive forces, and Greer's intelligence suggests they're expecting trouble." She pulled out the tablet with the surveillance footage, noting how Aaron's expression grew troubled as he studied the compound's layout.

"This looks like a fortress designed specifically to withstand siege. Multiple defensive perimeters, overlapping fields of fire, choke-points that would channel attackers into kill zones." He highlighted specific features on the tactical display. "Taking this place will require more than a small team operation. We'll need significant firepower and coordination."

"Then it's fortunate that I've been building a network of supernatural allies who specialize in exactly that kind of operation." Lily's voice cut through their conversation as she materialized from the cave system's deeper chambers, followed by figures who radiated the same dangerous competence as Aaron himself.

The reinforcements looked like they'd stepped out of a special operations manual—diverse ages and backgrounds, but all carrying themselves with the controlled violence of people who had learned to fight beings that operated beyond normal human limitations. Some were obviously Scions, their supernatural signatures marking them as children of various gods. Others felt different, enhanced in ways that suggested technological or mystical augmentation.

"Alexis Rain," Lily continued, "meet the core team that's been preparing for this operation since we learned about Phthonos's goals. Ex-military specialists who've adapted their skills for supernatural warfare, Scions who've chosen to fight rather than hide, and a few allies whose backgrounds are classified for everyone's protection."

A tall woman with silver-streaked hair stepped forward, her bearing suggesting command authority despite the absence of visible rank insignia. "Commander Sarah Mitchell, formerly U.S. Army Special Forces, currently leading a joint task force that doesn't officially exist." Her handshake was firm and brief. "I understand you're the primary intelligence asset for this operation."

"I have current surveillance data and facility layouts. What I don't have is detailed information about defensive capabilities or personnel strength." Alexis brought up the tactical displays Greer had provided, noting how the military specialists began annotating them with professional assessment. Out of everything they found, there was one blind-spot. One particular avenue of possible entry. "This feels off," Alexis noted. "Phthonos is a god who's survived for millennia by out-thinking his enemies. Pretty doubtful he would leave his primary facility vulnerable to any kind of assault we're planning."

"Unless he wants us to attack," Aaron said quietly. "Unless this is another trap designed to draw us into a situation where he controls all the variables."

"That's certainly possible. But we can't let paranoia paralyze us when time is running short." Mitchell studied the compound's defenses with the kind of systematic attention that came from years of planning similar operations. "Sometimes you have to accept calculated risks because the alternative is accepting defeat."

"What kind of timeline are we working with?" another specialist asked—a young man whose supernatural signature marked him as divine heritage despite his military bearing.

"Hours. Maybe a day, if we're lucky." Alexis thought about the Fates' warnings, about cosmic patterns that required precise timing and careful coordination. "The Restoration Protocol is moving toward implementation. Once Phthonos has what he needs from Jamie, he'll begin the process of rewriting universal law."

"Then we move tonight," Mitchell decided. "Coordinated assault, multiple entry points, overwhelming force applied at the most vulnerable positions." She began assigning roles and responsibilities with the efficiency of someone who had planned similar operations before. "But there's something you should understand about this mission."

"Which is?"

"This isn't a rescue operation. This is a war. The moment we breach that compound's perimeter, we'll be committed to total victory or total defeat. There won't be any middle ground, any negotiated settlement, any opportunity to withdraw if things go badly." Mitchell's expression grew grim. "Everyone who enters that facility needs to be prepared for the possibility that they won't be coming out."

The weight of that statement settled over the assembled team like a heavy cloak of truth. Not just risk, but near-certainty of casualties. Not just danger, but the kind of operation where success was measured in acceptable losses rather than perfect outcomes.

"Understood," Alexis said, speaking for the group. "When do we leave?"

"Transport lifts off in four hours. That gives us time for final equipment checks, communications protocols, and last-minute intelligence updates." Mitchell moved to a tactical display that showed the compound from multiple angles. "But first, there's something else you need to know about this facility."

"What?"

"It's not just a research center. These intelligence reports you've obtained suggest it's been configured as some kind of mystical laboratory. The kind of setup that could theoretically harness enough power that, if compromised, could likely destroy anything and everything within a wide radius."

The description made Alexis's blood run cold. Great. One more thing to worry about. Not blowing them all sky high.

The complex was not just imprisonment for Jamie, but transformation into a component in highly volatile cosmic machinery. His oracle abilities would be used as an interface between Phthonos's will and the Book of Fates.

"Can we disable it? Shut down whatever process they're using?"

"Unknown. The mystical components are beyond our technical expertise, and we won't know the full scope of what we're dealing with until we're inside the facility." Mitchell's expression grew troubled. "But there's something else. Something that changes the operational parameters significantly."

"Now what?"

"The facility isn't just defended by conventional forces. Intelligence suggests the presence of multiple divine beings, individuals with power levels that make normal supernatural threats seem trivial." She highlighted specific areas of the compound where mystical energy readings spiked beyond measurement. "Taking this place will require more than military tactics. It will require someone capable of engaging gods in direct combat."

All eyes turned to Alexis, and she felt the weight of cosmic responsibility settling around her like lead armor. Not just leadership, but the expectation that she could face beings who had shaped reality itself and emerge victorious.

"I'll handle the divine opposition," she said, power beginning to build beneath her skin in response to her emotional state. "Everyone else focuses on getting to Jamie and disrupting whatever process they're using to access the Book of Fates."

"And if you can't handle multiple gods simultaneously?" Aaron looked at her with an expression that exuded trust but concern. A little slip from him that she would hold onto for future reference.

"Then we improvise." She stood, moving toward the equipment lockers where specialized weapons waited for distribution. "But either way, we're going in. Because the alternative is letting Phthonos rewrite reality according to his personal preferences. Which means we all likely go bye-bye." There were few groans from the crowd. And a few deep inhalations at having that little nugget of information reinforced.

The next four hours passed in a blur of preparation and planning. Weapons cleaned, double and triple-checked and loaded, communication systems tested, mystical protections distributed to team members who lacked natural supernatural defenses. The kind of methodical preparation that increased survival odds in operations where survival was far from guaranteed.

Alexis found herself studying the tactical displays with growing unease. The compound's defenses were extensive but not insurmountable, its layout complex but navigable with proper coordination. Everything about the facility suggested it could be taken by a determined assault force with the right combination of firepower and supernatural abilities.

Too easy. The thought echoed through her mind as transport helicopters lifted them into the Canadian night, carrying them toward what might be their final battle. Phthonos was manipulating events again, engineering circumstances that would serve his purposes regardless of their apparent success or failure.

Still. Jamie was running out of time, and the cosmic knowledge the Fates had provided was burning through her consciousness like acid. Whatever trap Phthonos had prepared, whatever price he intended them to pay for their victory, it was too late to change course now.

The helicopters swept low over Lake Huron's dark waters, approaching the compound with the kind of tactical precision that came from years of similar operations. Below them, the industrial complex blazed with security lighting that made the surrounding forest look like a black ocean.

"One minute to insertion," Mitchell's voice crackled through their communication system. "Final equipment checks, confirm communications, prepare for immediate combat upon touchdown."

Alexis felt power building beneath her skin as the facility grew larger in their approach, mystical energy responding to proximity to enemies who had taken everything she cared about. The pendant the Fates had given her pulsed with cosmic knowledge that threatened to overwhelm her human consciousness, showing her glimpses of futures that branched and twisted according to choices she hadn't made yet. She had been careful not to mention the gift of the Fates. It would be on her to make the right choices... Even if they were not optimal to all involved. She steeled herself to what was to come.

The compound's defensive systems came online as they crossed the perimeter, automated weapons tracking their approach with mechanical precision. But instead of the devastating barrage she'd expected, only token resistance met their insertion— enough to maintain the illusion of defended territory without actually threatening their assault force.

"Too easy," Aaron said over the communications channel, echoing her own thoughts. "This feels like walking into an invitation rather than an attack."

"Could be overconfidence. Could be a trap. Could be that we're better than they expected." Mitchell's voice carried the kind of professional calm that came from accepting uncertainty as a tactical constant. "Either way, we're committed now. Execute the mission as planned and adapt to whatever we encounter."

The helicopters settled onto the compound's outer perimeter, disgorging assault teams that moved with practiced coordination toward their assigned objectives. Alexis felt the familiar tingle of accessing the ether, preparing to step between dimensions as soon as they encountered serious resistance.

But the resistance never came. Security forces that should have responded to their breach were absent or eliminated. Mystical wards that should have prevented supernatural infiltration failed to activate. Defensive systems that intelligence reports had described as cutting-edge remained silent and dark.

"Something's wrong," she said into her microphone. "This whole facility feels like a stage set. Like we're being guided toward a specific destination."

"The central laboratory," Aaron confirmed, studying readings from mystical sensors that tracked supernatural energy. "All the power signatures are concentrated in the main complex. Whatever they're doing with your friend, it's happening there."

Which meant they were walking exactly where Phthonos wanted them to go, following a script he'd written for purposes they didn't understand. But Jamie was in that central laboratory, trapped in whatever mystical interface was being used to access the Book of Fates.

Sometimes, even when you knew you were walking into a trap, you had to spring it anyway.

Because the alternative was leaving the people you loved to die alone.

CHAPTER 21: BROTHER VS. SISTER

Alexis made her move. She stepped into the ether, and exited directly inside the central laboratory.

The lab stretched across the compound's heart like a technological cathedral, its vaulted ceiling disappearing into shadows that seemed to move independently of any light source. Banks of servers hummed with processing power that felt more mystical than electronic, while displays showed data streams that hurt to look at directly—information that existed on levels human consciousness wasn't designed to process.

But it was the structure at the room's center that made Alexis's divine heritage recoil in recognition and terror.

The Oneiric Interface—the name came to her as if transmitted by the Fates' pendant—rose thirty feet into the air, a crystalline matrix that pulsed with energies that existed beyond normal space-time. Within its translucent depths, Jamie floated suspended like a specimen in amber, his body motionless but his eyes moving rapidly beneath closed lids. Cables and conduits connected him to machinery that disappeared into dimensions she couldn't perceive, while mystical symbols carved into the crystal's surface blazed with power that made her teeth ache.

"Beautiful, isn't it?" Phthonos's voice echoed through the laboratory with the satisfaction of an artist unveiling his masterpiece. "The perfect fusion of divine artifacts, mortal consciousness, and cosmic necessity. Your Oracle friend has become the key that will unlock universal revision itself."

He materialized from shadow near the Interface's base, no longer bothering with the facade of mortality he'd maintained during their previous encounters. Power radiated from him like heat from a forge, and his eyes held the malevolent intention that was genocide.

But it wasn't Phthonos that made her divine blood freeze with recognition. It was the artifact floating above the Interface's apex—a book bound in materials that predated creation itself, its pages containing text that shifted and writhed like living things.

The Book of Fates. The source code of reality itself.

"You recognize it," Phthonos said, noting her expression with obvious satisfaction. "The Moirai's greatest creation, containing the fundamental algorithms that govern existence, itself. Most beings can't even look at it without going insane. But you're not most beings, are you, sister?"

"Let him go." Power built beneath her skin, silver fire beginning to leak through her carefully maintained control. "Jamie has nothing to do with your war against Scions."

"On the contrary, he has everything to do with it. Your friend is the son of Apollo and Cassandra—the only combination of divine heritage capable of reading the Book's contents without being destroyed by the knowledge it contains." Phthonos gestured toward the Interface, where mystical energies flowed between Jamie's unconscious form and the floating artifact. "Even now, his oracle abilities are deciphering the laws that govern reality itself."

"Deciphering them for what?"

"Revision. Correction. The systematic elimination of every cosmic mistake that threatens universal stability." His smile carried the satisfaction of someone who had finally achieved a goal pursued for centuries. "Once I have complete access to the Book's contents, I can rewrite the fundamental structure of existence. Remove the law that allows divine and mortal blood to mix. Ensure that aberrations like you never existed in the first place."

The scope of his plan was clear, of course. Not just genocide of existing Scions, but retroactive erasure of their very existence from the timeline itself. The complete elimination of an entire category of beings from the fundamental structure of reality.

"That's impossible. Even gods can't rewrite universal law." She was biding her time, keeping him talking while she scanned everything in the room, everything to do with the interface. Hoping desperately for some clue as to how to stop this.

"Gods can't. But the Book of Fates can." He moved closer to the Interface, his presence making the mystical energies pulse with increased intensity. "Written by the Moirai before time had meaning, it contains the basic code that shapes everything—physics, causality, the boundaries between life and death. Change that code, and you change everything."

She thought about the Fates' warning, about patterns that served purposes greater than individual desire. They'd known this moment would come, had prepared her for a choice that would define the future of existence itself.

"The process is nearly complete," Phthonos continued, studying readouts that showed Jamie's neural activity interfacing with cosmic forces. "Your friend has been most cooperative, though I don't think he realizes what his compliance is facilitating. Soon, he'll provide the final authorization needed to begin universal revision."

"Authorization for what?"

"Retroactive elimination of divine-mortal hybrids from the timeline. One moment, Scions will exist throughout history. The next, they will never have existed at all. Reality will remember only pure bloodlines, stable genetics, the cosmic order as it was meant to be." His expression grew beatific. "No more aberrations. No more threats to universal stability. No more children who inherit powers they can't control and inevitably use to destroy everything around them."

The casual description of cosmic erasure made rage build in her chest like a nuclear fire. Everyone like her, everyone who might someday be like her, simply gone. As if they had never been born, never lived, never mattered to anyone.

"You're insane."

"I'm correct. And in approximately seventeen minutes, when the Interface completes its current cycle, I'll have proof that cosmic law agrees with my assessment." He gestured toward the Book of Fates, where text continued to shift and change as Jamie's consciousness interfaced with its contents. "The universe itself will validate the necessity of your elimination."

"What if it doesn't? What if the Book shows that Scions serve a purpose you're too blind to see?"

"Then I'll rewrite that section as well." His smile turned sharp and predatory. "The advantage of having access to fundamental reality, sister, is that you can correct any inconvenient truths you encounter."

The statement revealed the full scope of his megalomaniacal ambition. Not just the elimination of Scions, but the reshaping of cosmic law according to his personal preferences. The transformation of universal order into a reflection of his own prejudices and fears.

It was then that Alexis realized how quiet everything seemed. Something else was wrong.

"The assault team," she said, noting the absence of sounds that should have indicated ongoing combat. "Where are they?"

"Contained. Neutralized. Serving as additional motivation for your Oracle friend's cooperation, should he prove reluctant to complete his assigned task." Phthonos's expression grew smug. "Did you really think I hadn't anticipated your rescue attempt? That I would leave my most important operation vulnerable to the kind of direct assault you specialize in?"

"They're alive?"

"For now. Their continued existence depends on your friend's willingness to facilitate the final phase of universal revision." He moved to a control panel that displayed biometric readings for multiple individuals. "Though I should mention that their life support systems are tied to the Interface's operational parameters. Any attempt to disrupt the process will result in their immediate termination."

The threat was clear, calculated to paralyze her with moral conflict. Save Jamie and doom everyone else, or protect the assault team and allow cosmic erasure to proceed. The kind of impossible choice that had no good answers.

But as she studied the Interface's structure, noting the flow of mystical energy between its components, Alexis realized that Phthonos had made a critical error. The system was designed to prevent external interference, but it wasn't protected against someone who could access the ether directly.

"You're right about one thing," she said, power beginning to build toward critical mass beneath her skin. "I am an aberration. Something that shouldn't exist according to traditional cosmic law."

"Finally, you begin to understand—"

"I understand that you're afraid." Silver fire exploded from her in waves that made reality itself groan under the strain. "Afraid of change, afraid of evolution, afraid of a universe that might not need your kind of cosmic fascism to maintain stability."

She accessed the ether, stepping between dimensions to appear beside the Interface's crystalline matrix. But instead of trying to disrupt the machinery directly, she reached for Jamie's consciousness—the oracle abilities that were currently interfacing with the Book of Fates.

The connection blazed through her nervous system like liquid lightning, divine heritage recognizing divine heritage across the barriers of technology and mystical manipulation. For a moment, she existed in two places simultaneously—her physical form in the laboratory, her consciousness floating in whatever cosmic space Jamie's mind was navigating.

Alexis? His mental voice carried relief mixed with terror, the sound of someone who had been lost in darkness and finally heard a familiar voice. *I can't stop it. The Interface, it's using my abilities to read things that shouldn't be read, to access knowledge that's too dangerous for any mind to contain.*

Then we stop it together, she replied, channeling her power through their shared connection. *Show me what you're seeing.*

Images flooded her consciousness—the fundamental structure of reality laid bare, cosmic laws displayed as elegant equations that governed everything from quantum mechanics to divine politics. The Book of Fates wasn't just a repository of information—it was a living document that shaped existence through the simple act of recording it.

And there, highlighted in mystical fire that burned with Phthonos's envy and resentment, were the sections he intended to rewrite. Not just the laws that allowed divine-mortal mixing, but broader principles that governed cosmic diversity, evolutionary change, the very possibility of growth beyond established patterns.

He's not just targeting Scions, Jamie's consciousness whispered through their connection. *He's trying to lock the universe into stasis, to prevent any change that might threaten the existing power structure.*

Can you stop him?

Not alone. The Interface has too much control over my abilities. But together... together we might be able to redirect the process.

How?

Oracle abilities work both ways. I can read the future, but I can also speak it into existence under the right circumstances. If I can access Cassandra's gift instead of Apollo's sight...

Understanding blazed through her divine heritage like revelation. Cassandra's curse—true prophecy that was never believed. Jamie could speak the words that would prevent universal revision, but only if Phthonos did *not* believe them. Only if the god's own arrogance and certainty became the mechanism of his defeat.

But first, she had to buy them time.

Alexis withdrew from the ether back into normal reality, where Phthonos was studying Interface readouts with growing satisfaction, unconcerned with Alexis' presence by the machine. He could see that she had not attempted to prevent the machine's activities. She only appeared to be observing. Nothing had changed. The Book of Fates pulsed with energy that hurt to perceive directly, its pages turning of their own accord as cosmic revision approached critical mass.

"Thirteen minutes," he announced. "Then reality becomes what it should have been all along—stable, pure, free from the chaos that your kind represents."

"You're wrong about one thing," she said, power building toward explosive release. "I'm not just an aberration."

"No?"

"I'm the daughter of Nyx who's finally learned to stop holding back." She let the full weight of her divine heritage flood through her, silver fire exploding from her skin in waves that made the laboratory's mystical defenses scream and fail. "I'm the nightmare that keeps ancient gods awake at night."

The battle that followed was fought on levels that normal physics couldn't contain. Phthonos met her assault with cosmic forces that had existed since the dawn of creation, envy and resentment given form and focused into weapons that could unmake reality itself. But Alexis fought with the primal fury of someone defending everything she had left to lose, channeling powers that predated the universe he was trying to preserve.

They crashed through the laboratory's equipment, trading blows that would have shattered continents, while the Interface continued its countdown toward universal revision. Mystical energy blazed between them like captive stars, and the air itself began to breakdown under the pressure of primordial conflict.

Pitts was no slouch in the battle arena. His powers equaled Alexis' and he used them with eons of experience. Alexis made an attempt to land a roundhouse kick, only to receive a sharp stab in her solar plexus, knocking her to the floor. The force slid her twenty feet and she stumbled as she tried to regain her feet.

Pitts moved with ethereal grace and Alexis felt his blow, a fist to the jaw, with all the momentum he'd intended. Such a blow would have killed a large man. Alexis was no man. She fought to regain her senses, as the world waved at her as if melting and reforming. She was on her knees as Pitts lifted her and physically hurled her across the room. She hit the concrete floor and slammed into the wall enough to knock the breath from her chest.

"I expected more, really," Pitts commented as he strolled toward her for another attack. Alexis made for the ether, only to realize that all of the mystical enchantments and protocols that had been put in place made it feel like trying to dance in peanut butter. She fell back against the wall and quickly focused all her energy into healing. She felt Pitts' hand around her throat

Alexis felt the weightlessness for a moment as he lofted her, again, across the room. With a crashing thud, she landed directly against machines lined up against the far wall. She caught her breath and wondered how much more damage she could take.

Now, Jamie's voice whispered through their shared connection. *While he's distracted. I can access Cassandra's gift, but only for a moment.*

Alexis gathered all of her strength and threw everything she had at Phthonos, cosmic force meeting cosmic force in a collision that sent shock waves through dimensional barriers. She held little back, making sure that Pitts would concerned with little more than surviving her attack. For a crucial instant, the god's attention was completely focused on her assault, his certainty in eventual victory absolute and unshakeable.

Which was when Jamie quietly spoke the words that would save reality itself:

"The revision will fail. The Book of Fates will reject your commands. Universal law will remain unchanged, and Scions will continue to exist throughout time."

Phthonos barely registered the Oracle's pronouncement, his consciousness locked in combat with Alexis's primordial fury. But the Book of Fates heard every word, and Cassandra's curse ensured they carried the weight of absolute truth.

The mystical energies building toward cosmic revision suddenly reversed, fundamental forces recoiling from the impossibility of implementing changes that violated prophetic decree. The Interface's crystalline matrix began to crack and fracture as power levels spiked beyond its capacity to contain, while alarms shrieked warnings about catastrophic system failure.

"What did you do?" Phthonos screamed, his assault faltering as he realized the magnitude of what had just occurred.

"What I had to." Alexis channeled the full weight of night itself, drawing on powers that existed beyond the boundaries of normal space-time.

When she was young, just before her twelfth birthday, her father had arrived home from work and was shocked and frightened by the sight of his young daughter sitting confidently on the roof of their two-story home. He had had some choice words for her, forbidding her to climb up there again. It was far too dangerous. Yet, the strange thing was, not a week later, Alexis came home from school and saw that her father had built a very comfortable looking perch on the roof, with solid-built stairs leading from her bedroom window to the perch. She never questioned it. She just took to it like it was always there. Spending hours a night, lost in thought, basking in the darkness of night and the distant warmth of starlight.

She realized now that Nyx had apparently made contact with her father. *Never keep her from me.* Those were the words her father had mentioned Nyx had relayed. She'd been watching. She had always been watching. Watching her daughter grow, consume knowledge, love, build friendships, relationships. She watched from a distance as her daughter lived her life, surrounded by people who supported and loved her. And, that had made all the difference in the world.

Darkness flowed through her like liquid starlight, transforming her from a confused teenager into something that could challenge gods directly. "You thought I was so easily manipulated. You thought your plans and devious methods could break me. Let me tell you something, brother… You cannot and will not break the night."

The cosmic forces she unleashed weren't meant to destroy—they were meant to contain, to wrap around Phthonos's divine essence like chains forged from primordial authority. She drew on all of her power, her anger, her desire for vengeance and retribution and justice. And, with that, she focused all of her energy and brought down the literal weight of night upon him. But, even as darkness bound him, even as his grand plan collapsed into failure, she faced the choice that would define her moral character forever.

Destruction or mercy. Vengeance or justice. The kind of decision that would echo through eternity regardless of which path she chose.

Phthonos knelt before her, wrapped in shadows that could unmake his divine existence with a thought. His eyes held the shock of someone who had never doubted his own righteousness, who couldn't understand how cosmic necessity had failed to validate his actions.

"Do it," he whispered. "Complete your transformation. Become the monster they all fear and prove that my warnings about your kind were justified."

The temptation was overwhelming. He had killed her parents, orchestrated Jamie's torture, planned the systematic elimination of everyone like her. Justice demanded his destruction, and she had the power to deliver it with cosmic authority.

But as she looked at her half-brother—broken, defeated, consumed by envy that had shaped him into something monstrous—Alexis realized that destroying him, even if she could, would only validate his philosophy. That choosing vengeance over mercy would prove his point about Scions being too dangerous to exist.

"No," she said, the darkness around them shifting from weapon to sanctuary. "You don't get to make me into what you think I am."

"Then what?"

"Then someone else decides your fate. Someone with more authority than either of us." She felt cosmic attention turning toward their conflict, ancient powers taking notice of the daughter of Nyx who had chosen mercy over destruction. "Because this decision is too important for a teenager to make alone."

As if summoned by her words, the laboratory's shadows began to deepen and expand, darkness flowing through dimensions to announce the arrival of something vast and patient and utterly alien.

Nyx herself was coming.

And when she arrived, the real reckoning would begin.

CHAPTER 22: ORACLE AWAKENED

The darkness that flowed into the laboratory wasn't the absence of light—it was presence itself, ancient and vast and utterly alien to mortal comprehension. Shadows deepened beyond any natural phenomenon, becoming doorways through which something fundamental to existence could step from cosmic realms into the fragile reality of steel and concrete.

Nyx materialized from that primordial darkness like night given form and consciousness, her presence making the laboratory feel insignificant and temporary. She was tall—impossibly tall—with skin that held the depth of starless space and hair that moved like solar wind through cosmic void. Her eyes, which seemed to hold small galaxies swirling with impossible intent, contained the accumulated wisdom of eons, patient and terrible and completely beyond human understanding.

When she spoke, her voice carried the air of forces that had shaped reality itself. The very sound of it resonated in Alexis' bones.

"Phthonos."

The single word struck her son like a physical blow, divine authority crackling through syllables that had been spoken since the dawn of creation. He looked up from where Alexis's shadows still held him, his expression cycling between defiance and something that might have been relief.

"Mother," he replied, the title carrying years of accumulated resentment. "Come to witness my failure? To gloat over the collapse of necessary action?"

"Come to collect a child who has forgotten his purpose." Nyx moved closer, her presence making the air itself seem to thicken with cosmic weight. "You were never meant to reshape reality according to personal preference, Phthonos. You were meant to serve as a reminder that envy destroys rather than creates."

"They are aberrations! Cosmic mistakes that threaten universal stability!"

"They are evolution. Growth. The natural development of forces that have been building since your birth." Her gaze shifted to Alexis, and for a moment divine mother regarded divine daughter with something that might have been pride. "And this one has proven that your fears were groundless."

"She killed Harsh! She eliminated—"

"She chose mercy over vengeance when given the opportunity to destroy you completely." Nyx's voice carried the finality of absolute judgment. "The daughter of night understands what the god of envy has forgotten—that power without wisdom is meaningless, that strength without compassion creates only emptiness."

Phthonos struggled against the shadows that bound him, his divine nature railing against the cosmic sentence he could feel approaching. "And what of the Restoration Protocol? What of the threat Scions represent to—"

"Enough." The word rang through dimensions, silencing his protests with primordial authority. "You will be confined, Phthonos. Not destroyed, not eliminated, but removed from circumstances where your envy can cause further damage. Consider it a timeout of cosmic proportions."

She gestured, and darkness deeper than the space between stars opened beneath the bound god. Not a portal to destruction, but to somewhere else—a realm where divine beings could contemplate their errors without threatening the stability of existence itself.

"How long?" Phthonos asked as the void began to claim him.

"Until you learn the difference between necessary action and personal vendetta. Until you understand that diversity strengthens rather than weakens the cosmic order." Nyx's expression softened slightly. "I still love you, my son. But love does not excuse the choices you have made."

He disappeared into cosmic darkness, his divine essence transported to whatever realm served as prison for gods who had forgotten their purpose. The laboratory fell silent except for the dying hum of damaged equipment and the sound of mystical energies slowly dissipating.

Alexis felt the weight of cosmic attention focusing on her, ancient intelligence evaluating her choices and their consequences. Meeting her divine mother should have been overwhelming, the culmination of eighteen years of questions about her true heritage. Instead, it felt strangely natural—like returning to something that had always been part of her.

"Hello, daughter."

"Hello, mother." The words came easier than she'd expected. "Thank you for—"

"You handled the situation correctly. Mercy was the appropriate choice, even though vengeance would have been more satisfying." Nyx moved to the Oneiric Interface, where Jamie remained suspended in crystalline matrix that was beginning to crack and fracture. "But your friend paid a considerable price for accessing knowledge no mortal mind was designed to contain."

The Interface suddenly shattered, its mystical components unable to maintain coherence now that the Book of Fates had rejected Phthonos's commands. Jamie tumbled from the collapsing matrix, his body hitting the laboratory floor with the boneless impact of someone whose consciousness existed somewhere far from physical reality.

Alexis bolted to his side, kneeling by his motionless form while checking for vital signs that were growing weaker by the moment. His pulse was thready and irregular, his breathing shallow and labored. Worse, his eyes moved beneath closed lids with the rapid motion that suggested his mind was still partially interfaced with cosmic forces that could tear human consciousness apart.

"He's dying," Alexis said, power building beneath her skin as divine healing abilities responded to her emotional state. "The Interface damaged something fundamental. I can feel his life force fading."

"The price of accessing knowledge beyond mortal comprehension," Nyx replied, her voice carrying the weight of cosmic law rather than maternal concern. "Oracle abilities allow limited interface with divine information. But what your friend experienced went far beyond those limitations."

"Can you help him?"

"Divine law restricts direct intervention in mortal affairs. Even this conversation violates protocols that could result in cosmic censure." Nyx's expression grew troubled. "But there may be another way. If he can awaken his divine heritage sufficiently to heal himself..."

"How? He's unconscious, barely breathing. How is he supposed to access abilities he doesn't even know he has?"

"Through connection to someone whose power can serve as a bridge. Someone who loves him enough to risk their own divine essence to save his life." Nyx's gaze fixed on Alexis with laser intensity. "Are you prepared to make that sacrifice, daughter?"

The question hung in the air between them like a loaded weapon. Not just risk, but potential loss of everything that made her more than human. The possibility of burning out her divine heritage to save Jamie's life.

Before she could answer, the temperature in the laboratory dropped twenty degrees in the span of a heartbeat. Frost began forming on the broken equipment, while shadows that had nothing to do with Nyx's presence began gathering in the far corners of the room. The sound of hooves announced his approach.

Death had come calling.

Thanatos materialized from those unnatural shadows like inevitability given form—tall, pale, carrying himself with the patient dignity of someone whose work was both necessary and eternal. His eyes held the compassion of someone who understood that ending was often mercy, but also the implacable certainty of cosmic law.

"The Oracle's time has come," he said, his voice carrying finality that could end worlds. "His consciousness has been damaged beyond repair. Natural law requires that I collect what remains before further deterioration occurs."

"No." Alexis stood between Death and Jamie's unconscious form, power building toward levels that made reality itself groan under the strain. "You're not taking him."

"I am not taking anyone. I am fulfilling my function as ordained by cosmic necessity." Thanatos moved closer, his presence making the air itself seem to thin and grow cold. "The mortal who accessed divine knowledge beyond his capacity to contain has paid the price for that transgression. To allow continued existence in his current state would be cruelty rather than kindness."

"He's not just mortal. He's a Scion, son of Apollo and Cassandra. He has divine heritage that should protect him from this kind of damage."

"Heritage that remains unwakened, potential that was never properly developed. Without active divine power to sustain his consciousness, what remains is a body whose soul has been scattered across cosmic dimensions." Death's expression softened slightly. "I understand your attachment, sister. But some losses cannot be prevented through force of will alone."

"Then I'll awaken his heritage myself." She knelt beside Jamie again, reaching for the connection they'd shared through the Interface's mystical network. "Bridge his consciousness back to his body through direct power transfer."

"The risk—" Nyx began.

"Is mine to take." Alexis placed her hands on Jamie's chest, feeling the weak flutter of his heartbeat against her palms. "He saved reality itself by speaking the words that stopped Phthonos's revision. I'm not letting Death claim him as payment for cosmic heroism."

She reached deep into her divine heritage, accessing power that existed beyond the boundaries of normal space-time. Silver fire flowed from her hands into Jamie's motionless form, not healing in any conventional sense but serving as a bridge that could guide scattered consciousness back to its physical anchor.

The process was agonizing, like trying to hold lightning in her bare hands while navigating cosmic forces that could unmake mortal minds. But she felt Jamie's consciousness responding, fragments of his essential self, beginning to coalesce around the lifeline she was providing.

Alexis? His mental voice was weak but growing stronger. *Where... what happened to the Interface?*

Gone. Destroyed. Phthonos has been dealt with. She poured more power into the connection, feeling her own life force beginning to strain under the demands of sustaining them both. *But you need to wake up. Your body is shutting down, and I can't maintain this bridge much longer.*

I can't. Something's wrong. I can see the divine power, feel it trying to respond, but it's like trying to crank over an engine that's missing its starter.

Understanding blazed through her exhausted consciousness. Jamie's divine heritage was intact but inactivated, potential that required an external trigger to become functional reality. But that trigger would have to come from someone whose bloodline connected to his own.

"Apollo," she gasped, speaking to the laboratory around her. "If you can hear this, your son needs you. Now."

Light blazed through the damaged facility—not the harsh glare of electrical illumination but the warm radiance of summer sunlight concentrated into divine presence. Apollo materialized beside Jamie's unconscious form, his perfect features twisted with concern and guilt that had been building for eighteen years.

"I'm here," he said, kneeling beside his son while power flowed from his hands in golden streams. "I should have been here before. Should have been watching, protecting, preparing him for this kind of cosmic responsibility."

"Later," Alexis managed, her own strength fading as the power transfer continued. "Right now, just help me wake up his heritage."

Apollo's divine energy joined with hers, solar radiance combining with primordial darkness to form something that transcended both sources. The power flowed into Jamie's body with the intensity of controlled fusion, awakening potential that had been dormant since birth.

His eyes snapped open, blazing with golden light that spoke of prophetic sight awakening to its full potential. But more than that—healing abilities inherited from Apollo began working to repair the damage caused by interfacing with cosmic knowledge, while oracle gifts from Cassandra provided the wisdom needed to integrate divine and mortal consciousness safely.

"I can see," he whispered, his voice carrying harmonics that hadn't been there before. "Everything. Past, present, the branching paths of possible futures. And I understand... I understand what we prevented."

Thanatos stepped back, his cosmic authority recognizing that natural law no longer required intervention. "The Oracle lives. The debt has been paid through awakening rather than death." He bowed slightly to the assembled divine figures. "My services are no longer required."

He vanished into shadow, leaving behind only the lingering scent of winter air and the certainty that Jamie had passed beyond his reach—at least for now.

"How do you feel?" Alexis asked, exhaustion making her voice hoarse as she helped him sit up.

"Different. Like I've been carrying a weight I didn't know was there, and someone finally helped me set it down." Jamie studied his hands, where golden light still flickered beneath the skin. "I can feel the oracle abilities, but they're... controlled now. Integrated instead of overwhelming."

"Good." Apollo stood, his presence beginning to fade as he prepared to return to whatever realm divine law required him to inhabit. "But remember—power without wisdom is meaningless. Use your gifts responsibly, and never forget that being able to see the future doesn't mean you're obligated to accept it."

"I won't." Jamie looked from his father to Alexis, understanding passing between them that went beyond words. "Thank you. Both of you. For not giving up when it would have been easier to let go."

Nyx moved closer, her presence making the ruined laboratory feel like a temple to forces that predated creation. "The immediate crisis has been resolved. The Book of Fates has been secured, Phthonos has been contained, and cosmic balance has been restored. But this is only the beginning, daughter."

"Beginning of what?"

"Your role as guardian of the space between mortal and divine worlds. The Scions will need protection, guidance, someone who understands both heritage and responsibility." Her expression grew serious. "The cosmic community has taken notice of recent events. Decisions will be made about the future of mixed-blood children, and those decisions will be influenced by the precedent you have set today."

"What kind of precedent?"

"That power can be wielded without corruption. That divine heritage can serve justice rather than personal ambition. That children of gods can choose their own destinies rather than being bound by the expectations of others." Nyx's smile carried warmth that had been absent from their previous interactions. "You have proven that Scions are evolution rather than aberration, daughter. The question now is whether you are prepared to help others learn the same lesson."

The weight of cosmic responsibility settled on Alexis's shoulders, but it felt lighter than before—shared rather than carried alone. She looked at Jamie, whose awakened abilities were already providing glimpses of possible futures where Scions lived openly rather than in hiding, where divine heritage was celebrated rather than feared. He nodded with that slight smirk of his. Adorable.

"Yes," she said. "We're ready."

"Good." Nyx began to fade back into the primordial darkness from which she'd emerged. "Because the universe is about to become a much more interesting place."

As divine presence withdrew from the laboratory, leaving behind only mortal reality and the lingering scent of starlight, Alexis felt something fundamental shift in her understanding of the world. The war for Scion survival wasn't over—it was transformed into something larger and more hopeful.

For the first time since Elizabeth's death, the future felt like possibility rather than threat.

And that was enough to begin building something better.

CHAPTER 23: NEW BEGINNINGS

The abandoned camp in New Hampshire's White Mountains had been transformed into something that defied easy categorization—part military installation, part university campus, part sanctuary for beings who existed between worlds. Three weeks had passed since the confrontation in Ontario, three weeks of coordinating rescues, establishing safe houses, and building the infrastructure necessary to protect a community that had spent generations hiding in isolation.

Alexis stood on the central lodge's wraparound porch, watching dawn break over granite peaks while her enhanced senses monitored the dozen new arrivals who had found their way to the facility during the night. Each one carried the supernatural signature that marked divine heritage, refugees from a world that was slowly learning to acknowledge their existence.

"The Senate Intelligence Committee wants another briefing," Lily called from the communications center, her voice carrying the weary satisfaction of someone who had been fielding similar requests for days. "Apparently they're still having trouble processing the concept of gods walking among us."

"Tell them we'll consider it after they explain how they plan to classify information that half their staff already leaked to foreign intelligence services." Alexis moved inside, noting how the lodge's great room had been converted into a coordination center that surpassed anything she'd seen in Aaron's mountain facility. "Any word from the European networks?"

"Rose Hartford has been released from St. Anne's and is coordinating Scion identification efforts across the UK. Apparently, having the ability to see probability matrices makes her very effective at predicting which children will manifest abilities. Whatever your mother did for her seems to be working."

Lily pulled up real-time data streams that showed supernatural incidents reported across multiple continents. "The masquerade is completely broken now. Government agencies are scrambling to develop protocols for managing supernatural citizens."

"Managing or controlling?"

"Bit of both, probably. But the political landscape is shifting faster than anyone expected. Hard to maintain oppressive policies when your target population includes people who can step between dimensions or predict your next move with oracle-level accuracy."

Alexis studied the intelligence reports, noting patterns that suggested the systematic persecution of Scions was giving way to something more complex. Not acceptance—that would take generations—but recognition that extermination was no longer a viable option.

"Where's Keats?" she asked, realizing she hadn't seen him since the previous evening.

"Conference room three. Apollo arrived about an hour ago for what he called 'necessary conversations about divine family dynamics.'" Lily's expression grew troubled. "Though there was something strange about his arrival. He seemed... weaker somehow. Less radiant than usual."

The comment seemed to resonate with Alexis more than she couldn't quite explain. That would be something worth following up on. She'd grown accustomed to the overwhelming presence that divine beings projected, but now that Lily mentioned it, she'd noticed similar changes in other supernatural encounters recently.

The conference room felt charged with odd tension when Alexis entered. Apollo sat across from Jamie, but something was definitely different about the god's usual solar radiance. His light seemed dimmer, more flickering than steady, like a candle fighting against wind.

"How are you feeling?" Alexis asked Jamie, settling into one of the chairs while noting how both figures seemed more solid, more anchored to physical reality than she expected from divine beings.

"Different. Like I've been carrying a weight I didn't know was there, and someone finally helped me set it down." Jamie studied his hands, where golden light still flickered beneath the skin, though it too seemed less consistent than before. "The oracle abilities are controlled now, integrated instead of overwhelming."

"That's good." She reached over and took his hand, feeling the familiar warmth of connection that had sustained them through cosmic crises. "I was worried we might lose the parts of you that made you... you."

Their eyes met, and something passed between them that had been building since childhood but never quite acknowledged. The shared trials, the trust that ran deeper than friendship, the way they'd saved each other's lives and souls without question or hesitation.

"Alexis," Jamie said quietly, his voice carrying harmonics that hadn't been there before his awakening. "There's something I need to—"

She leaned forward and kissed him, simple and gentle but carrying eighteen years of friendship transformed into something deeper. When they broke apart, both were smiling with the kind of contentment that came from finally understanding something that had always been true.

"About time," Apollo murmured with paternal amusement, though his expression quickly grew serious again. "But we have more pressing matters to discuss. There have been... irregularities in divine communications recently."

"What kind of irregularities?" Alexis asked, though she was still processing the warmth of Jamie's hand in hers.

"Prayer responses are becoming inconsistent. Divine interventions that should be automatic are failing to manifest. Several of my siblings have reported difficulty maintaining their connections to mortal affairs." Apollo's diminished radiance flickered with concern. "At first, we assumed it was residual effects from the cosmic disruption Phthonos caused, but the pattern is growing worse rather than healing."

Jamie's oracle abilities suddenly blazed to life, his eyes filling with golden light as prophetic sight activated unbidden. "I see... something missing. Ancient things. Important things. Like..." He struggled for words. "Like someone's removing the bridges between worlds."

The vision faded, leaving him looking drained and confused. "I'm sorry. It's not clear yet. The sight keeps showing me empty spaces where something should be, but I can't identify what's missing."

"Empty spaces," Apollo repeated thoughtfully. "That's... troubling. Divine power flows through specific conduits, ancient artifacts that anchor our influence in the mortal realm. If something were happening to those conduits..."

He didn't finish the thought, but the implications hung heavy in the air. Without those connections, gods would become increasingly isolated in their own realms, unable to effectively help or influence mortals. And if the gods were cut off, what would happen to their Scion children?

"How long has this been happening?" Alexis asked.

"The reports started about two weeks ago, just scattered incidents that seemed unrelated. But the pattern is accelerating." Apollo stood, his movements carrying less of their usual effortless grace. "I came here partly to warn you, and partly to ask for your help."

"Our help with what?"

"Investigation. Your network has resources and perspectives that the divine community lacks. If someone is targeting the fundamental connections between divine and mortal realms, we need to identify the threat before the separation becomes irreversible."

The weight of cosmic responsibility was settling around Alexis again, but this time it felt different—shared rather than carried alone, purposeful rather than reactive. She looked at Jamie, whose oracle abilities were already providing glimpses of possible futures that seemed to shift and change even as he observed them.

"We'll look into it," she said. "But first, we need to understand exactly what we're dealing with."

Two months later

The situation had grown worse faster than anyone had anticipated.

Alexis stood in the main coordination center, watching real-time data feeds that painted an increasingly troubling picture. Prayer response rates had dropped to less than forty percent across all major pantheons. Divine inspirations—the source of breakthrough scientific discoveries, artistic masterpieces, and spiritual revelations—had virtually ceased. Most alarming of all, several Scions had begun experiencing power fluctuations that suggested their divine connections were weakening.

"Another artifact confirmed missing," Aaron reported from his workstation, where intelligence from supernatural communities worldwide painted a grim picture. "Demeter's original grain seeds. The ones that anchor her connection to harvest and growth."

"That makes seven in the past month." Alexis moved to the tactical display, where red markers indicated confirmed thefts of divine artifacts across multiple pantheons. "Apollo's first lyre, Hermes' sandals, Thor's original hammer Mjolnir before the one he carries now, Thoth's palette and brush, Amaterasu's sacred mirror..."

"And they're not random," Jamie added, his oracle abilities providing insights that made the pattern more disturbing. "Each one is a *connection* artifact—something that allows divine power to flow into the mortal world. Without them, the gods become increasingly isolated in their own realms."

"Any leads on who's behind it?"

"Whoever it is knows divine security intimately and has access to realms that should be impossible to breach." Aaron highlighted specific intelligence reports. "These aren't smash-and-grab operations. The thefts are surgical, precise, carried out by someone who understands exactly what they're taking and why."

The scope of the threat was staggering. Not just theft, but the severing of the connections that had existed between divine and mortal realms since the dawn of civilization.

"The really troubling part," Aaron continued, "is that we're getting reports of some of the original Smiths going missing. The Cyclopes, Wayland the Smith, even rumors that Ptah hasn't been seen in his usual haunts."

"The Smiths who forged the connection artifacts in the first place," Alexis said, drawing on her own interior questioning. "Someone doesn't just want to steal the artifacts—they want to understand how they work. How to destroy them permanently."

Discussions continued and although she was autonomously recording every word into her eidetic memory, Alexis was lost in her thoughts. The girl who had stood numb at her mother's funeral was gone, replaced by someone who understood that with power came responsibility, that strength was meaningless without wisdom, and that the future belonged to those brave enough to build it rather than waiting for it to happen.

But as she looked at Jamie, whose oracle abilities were already providing glimpses of the challenges ahead, and at the tactical displays showing their growing network of allies and resources, Alexis felt something she hadn't experienced in months.

Anticipation.

The next battle was before them. And for the first time since this all started, she was ready not just to react to threats, but to shape the outcome according to her own vision of what the universe could become.

Outside the coordination center, dawn broke over the White Mountains in streams of gold and crimson, painting the sky with the promise of possibilities yet to be explored. But somewhere in the growing light, ancient powers were stirring, preparing challenges that would test everything she had learned about power, responsibility, and the price of protecting the connections that bound worlds together.

The future stretched ahead like an unwritten book, its pages waiting to be filled with stories of courage, hope, and the eternal struggle between those who sought to divide worlds and those who fought to keep them connected.

It was going to be the adventure of a lifetime.

And she couldn't wait to begin.

ABOUT THE AUTHOR

C.L. Stegall is a versatile author of modern fiction whose imaginative storytelling spans multiple genres. His diverse portfolio includes the Young Adult **New Scions series** (beginning with *The Broken Night*), the Urban Fantasy **Valence of Infinity series**, thriller works such as *Fields of Anger*, and additional short stories available freely on his website.

Beyond his novels, Stegall has made significant contributions to the literary community as editor and contributor to acclaimed anthology collections, including *4POCALYPSE - Four Tales Of A Dark Future* and *4RCHETYPES Modern Interpretations of Classic Horror*. His expertise and passion for storytelling have made him a sought-after speaker at writers' conferences and workshops, where he generously shares his knowledge and experience with fellow writers.

Before pursuing his writing career, Stegall served ten years in the U.S. Army, where he worked as both an engineer and a Spanish linguist with Military Intelligence.

This military background, combined with his extensive travels throughout the Western Hemisphere, brings an authentic depth and global perspective to his work.

Born in North Carolina, Stegall knew from an early age that his world extended far beyond small-town boundaries. After graduating high school, he immediately enlisted in the Army, beginning a journey that would take him across multiple states and countries. His path eventually led him to California, where he met his wife, Mona, who has been his partner and biggest supporter for over 25 years.

A former President and Senior Editor at Dark Red Press, Stegall continues to be deeply involved in the publishing industry. When he's not writing, he pursues his other creative passions through Studio Valensi, where he works as a music producer and photographer alongside his wife.

Currently residing in Texas with Mona and their cat, Shoyu, he remains an avid fan of science fiction and fantasy in all their forms. He's also known among friends for his love of carrot cake and his commitment to supporting other writers in their creative journeys.

Stegall's work is characterized by its blend of mythological elements with contemporary settings, complex character development, and fast-paced storytelling that keeps readers engaged from beginning to end.

You can always find out more and enjoy some free reads at his website

http://CLStegall.com

COMING 2026!

NEW SCIONS: BOOK TWO

THE CHAOS ARENA